Enoch Arnold Bennett, the son of
in Hanley, Staffordshire. At twenty, ~~~,
initially to work as a solicitor's clerk, but he soon turned to
writing popular serial fiction and editing a women's magazine.
After the publication of his first novel, *A Man From the North*
in 1898, he became a professional writer. He moved to Paris and
became a man of cosmopolitan and discerning tastes.

Bennett's great reputation is built upon the success of his
novels and short stories set in the Potteries, an area of north
Staffordshire that he recreated as the 'Five Towns'. *Anna of the
Five Towns* and *The Old Wives' Tale* show the influence of
Flaubert, Maupassant and Balzac as Bennett describes provincial
life in great detail. Arnold Bennett is an important link between
the English novel and European realism. He wrote several plays
and lighter works such as *The Grand Babylon Hotel* and *The
Card*.

Arnold Bennett died in 1931.

BY THE SAME AUTHOR
ALL PUBLISHED BY HOUSE OF STRATUS

THE CLAYHANGER SERIES:
CLAYHANGER
HILDA LESSWAYS
THESE TWAIN
THE ROLL CALL

FIVE TOWNS SERIES:
A MAN FROM THE NORTH
ANNA OF THE FIVE TOWNS
THE CARD
THE OLD WIVES' TALE
THE REGENT
TALES OF THE FIVE TOWNS

FANTASIAS:
THE CITY OF PLEASURE
THE GHOST

NOVELS:
ACCIDENT
BURIED ALIVE
THE GLIMPSE
THE GRAND BABYLON HOTEL
LORD RAINGO
THE PRETTY LADY
RICEYMAN STEPS
TERESA OF WATLING STREET

NON-FICTION:
HOW TO LIVE ON 24 HOURS A DAY

The City of Pleasure

Arnold Bennett

HOUSE OF
STRATUS

Copyright Arnold Bennett; House of Stratus

All rights reserved. No part of this publication may be reproduced, stored in a retrieval system, or transmitted, in any form, or by any means (electronic, mechanical, photocopying, recording, or otherwise), without the prior permission of the publisher. Any person who does any unauthorised act in relation to this publication may be liable to criminal prosecution and civil claims for damages.

The right of Arnold Bennett to be identified as the author of this work has been asserted.

This edition published in 2002 by House of Stratus, an imprint of Stratus Books Ltd., 21 Beeching Park, Kelly Bray, Cornwall, PL17 8QS, UK. www.houseofstratus.com

Typeset, printed and bound by House of Stratus.

A catalogue record for this book is available from the British Library and the Library of Congress.

ISBN 07551-158-8-0

This book is sold subject to the condition that it shall not be lent, resold, hired out, or otherwise circulated without the publisher's express prior consent in any form of binding, or cover, other than the original as herein published and without a similar condition being imposed on any subsequent purchaser, or bona fide possessor.

This is a fictional work and all characters are drawn from the author's imagination. Any resemblances or similarities to persons either living or dead are entirely coincidental.

PART ONE

CARPENTARIA

1

OVER THE CITY

"Carpentaria!"

One of the three richly uniformed officials who were in charge of the captive balloon, destined to be a leading attraction of the City of Pleasure, murmured this name warningly to his companions, as if to advise them that the moment had arrived for them to mind their p's and q's. And each man looked cautiously through the tail of his eye at a striking figure which was approaching through crowds of people to the enclosure. The figure was tall and had red hair and a masterful face, and it was clothed in a blue suit that set off the red hair to perfection. Over the wicket of the enclosure a small enamelled sign had been hung:

"CITY OF PLEASURE.

"*President*: JOSEPHUS ILAM.

"*Managing and Musical Director* : CHARLES CARPENTARIA.

"Balloon Ascents every half-hour after three o'clock. Height of a thousand feet guaranteed. Seats, half-a-crown, including field-glass."

The sign was slightly askew, and the approaching figure tapped it into position, and then entered the enclosure.

"Good afternoon," it said. "Everything ready?"

"'d afternoon, Mr Carpentaria," said the head balloonist respectfully. "Yes, sir."

The three men with considerable ostentation busied themselves among ropes, while a young man in gold-rimmed spectacles gazed with sudden self-consciousness into the far distance, just as if he had that very instant discovered something there that demanded the whole of his attention.

"Going up, sir?" inquired the head balloonist.

"Yes," replied Carpentaria. "Mr Ilam and I are going up together. We have time, haven't we? It's only half-past two."

"Yes, sir."

Carpentaria examined the vast balloon, which was trembling and swaying and lugging with that aspiration towards heaven and the infinite so characteristic of well-filled balloons. He ignored the young man in spectacles.

"Where's the parachutist?" Carpentaria demanded.

A parachutist was to give *eclat* to the first public ascent of the silken monster by dropping from it into the Thames or somewhere else. His apparatus hung beneath the great circular car.

"He'll be here before three, sir," said the head balloonist.

"He's been here once, sir," added the second balloonist, anxious to prove to himself that he also had the right to converse with the mighty Carpentaria.

A few seconds later the august President arrived. Mr Josephus Ilam was tall, like his partner, but much stouter. He had, indeed, almost the inflated appearance which one observes constantly in the drivers of brewers' drays; even his fingers bulged. His age was fifty, ten years more than that of Carpentaria, and it was probably ten years since he had seen his own feet. Finally, he was clean-shaven, with areas of blue on his chin and cheeks like the sea on a map, and his hair – what remained of it – seemed to be hesitating between black and grey.

"What's the matter?" he asked of Carpentaria.

"Oh, I thought I would just like to make the first ascent with you alone," Carpentaria answered; and added, smiling, "I have something to show you up there."

His hand indicated the firmament, and his peculiar smile indicated that he took Ilam's consent for granted.

Ilam sighed obesely, and agreed. He did not care to argue before members of the staff. Nevertheless, the futility of ascending to the skies on this, the opening day, when the colossal organism of the show cried aloud for continual supervision on earth, was sufficiently clear to his mind. He climbed gingerly over the edge of the wickerwork car, which had a circumference of thirty feet, with a protected aperture in the middle, and Carpentaria followed him.

"Let go," said Carpentaria gleefully. "Let go!" he repeated with impatience, when the balloon was arrested at a height of about ten feet.

"Right, sir," responded briskly the head balloonist. There appeared to have been some altercation between the balloonists.

The day was the first of May, but the London spring had chosen to be capricious and unseasonable. Instead of the snow and frost and east wind which almost invariably accompany what is termed, with ferocious irony, the merry month, there was strong brilliant sunshine and a perfect calm. The sun glinted and glittered on the upper surfaces of the balloon, but of course the voyagers could not perceive that. They, in fact, perceived nothing except that the entire world was gradually falling away from them. The balloon had ceased to shiver; it stood as firm as consols, while the City of Pleasure sank and sank, and the upturned faces of more than fifty thousand spectators grew tinier and tinier.

It would be interesting and certainly instructive to unfold some of the many mysteries and minor dramas which had diversified the history of the making of the City of Pleasure, from the time when Carpentaria, having conceived the idea of the thing, found the necessary millionaire in the person of Josephus Ilam, to the hurried and tumultuous eve of the opening day; but these are unconnected with the present recital. It needs only to remind the reader of the City's geography. Towards the lower left-hand corner of any map of London not later than 1905, may be observed a large, nearly empty space in the form of an inverted letter "U." This space is bounded everywhere, except across the bottom, by the Thames. It is indeed a peninsula made by an extraordinary curve of the Thames, and Barnes Common connects it with the mainland of the parish of Putney. Its dimensions are little short of a mile either way, and yet, although Hammersmith Bridge joins it to Hammersmith at the top, it was almost uninhabited, save for the houses which lined Bridge Road and a scattering of houses in Lonsdale Road and the short streets between Lonsdale Road and the reservoir near the bridge. The contrast was violent ; on the north side of the Thames the crowded populousness of Hammersmith, and on the south side – well, possibly four people to the acre.

Ilam and Carpentaria, with Ilam's money, bought or leased the whole of the middle part of the peninsula – over three hundred acres – with a glorious half-mile frontage to the Thames on the east side. They would have acquired all the earth as far as Barnes Common but for the fact that the monomaniacs of the Ranelagh Club Golf Course could not be induced to part with their links, even when offered a fantastic number of thousand pounds per hole. They obtained the closing of the Bridge Road, which cut the peninsula downwards into two halves, and the omnibus traffic between Hammersmith and Barnes was diverted to Lonsdale Road – not without terrific diplomacy, and pitched battles in the columns of newspapers and in Local Government Offices. They pulled down every house in Bridge Road, thus breaking up some seventy presumably happy English homes, and then they Started upon the erection of the City of Pleasure, which they intended to be, and which all the world now admits to be, the most gigantic enterprise of amusement that Europe has ever seen.

As the balloon rose the general conformation of the City of Pleasure became visible. Running almost north and south from Hammersmith Bridge was the Central Way, the splendid private thoroughfare which had superseded Bridge Road. It was a hundred feet wide, and its surface was treated with westrumite, and a service of gaily coloured cable-cars flashed along it in either direction, between the north and the south entrances to the City. It was lined with multifarious buildings, all painted cream – the theatre, the variety theatre, the concert hall, the circus, the panorama, the lecture hall, the menagerie, the art gallery, the story-tellers' hall, the dancing-rooms, restaurants, cafés and bars, and those numerous shops for the sale of useless and expensive souvenirs without which the happiness of no Briton on a holiday is complete. The footpaths, twenty feet wide, were roofed with glass, and between the footpaths and the roadway came two rows of trees which were industriously taking advantage of the weather to put forth their verdure. Footpaths and road were thronged with people, and the street was made gay, not only by the toilettes and sunshades of women, but also by processions of elephants, camels, and other wild-fowl, bearing children of all ages in charge of gorgeous Indians and Ethiops. From every roof floated great crimson flags with the legend in gold: "City of Pleasure. President: Ilam; Director: Carpentaria." Add to this combined effect the music of bands and the sunshine, and do not forget the virgin creaminess of the elaborate architecture, and you will be able to form a notion of the spectacle offered by the esplanade upon which Ilam and Carpentaria looked down.

Midway between the north and south entrances, the Central Way expanded itself into a circular place, with a twenty-jetted bronze fountain in the middle. To the west was the facade of what was called the Exposition Palace, an enormous quadrangular building, containing a huge covered court which, with balconies, would hold twenty thousand people on wet days. The galleries of the palace were devoted to an exhibition of everything that related to woman, from high-heeled shoes to thrones; it was astonishing how many things did relate to woman. North of the Exposition Palace stretched out the Amusements Park, where people looped the loop, shot the shute, wheeled the wheel, switched the switchback, &c.; and here was the balloon enclosure. South of the palace lay the Sports Field, where a cricket match was progressing.

Finally, and most important of all, to the east of the circular place in Central Way rose the impressive entrance to the Oriental Gardens, the pride of Ilam and Carpentaria. The Oriental Gardens occupied the entire eastern side of the City, and they sloped down to the Thames. They formed over a hundred acres of gardens, wood, and pleasaunce, laid out with formal magnificence. Flowers bloomed there in defiance of seasons. On every hand the eye was met by vistas of trees and shrubs, and by lawns and statues, and lakes and fountains. In the middle was Carpentaria's own special bandstand. A terrace, two thousand five hundred feet long, bordered the river, and from the terrace jutted out a pier at which steamers were unloading visitors.

2

INTERVIEWED

The occupants of the balloon could see everything. They saw the debarkation from the steamers; they saw the unending crowd of doll-like persons thrown up out of the ground by the new Tube station at the south end of Hammersmith Bridge; they saw the heavy persistent stream of vehicles and pedestrians over the bridge; they saw the trains approaching Barnes on the South-Western Railway; they saw the struggles for admittance at all the gates of the City; they even saw flocks of people streaming Cityward along the Barnes High Street and the Lower Richmond Road. It was not for nothing that advertisements of the City of Pleasure had filled one solid page of every daily paper in London, and many in the provinces, for a week past. Visitors were now entering the City at the rate of seventy thousand an hour, at a shilling a head.

There was a gentle tug beneath the car. The thousand feet of rope had been paid out, and the balloon hung motionless.

Then a faint noise, something between the crackling of musketry and the surge of waves on a pebbly beach, ascended from the City.

"They're cheering," said Josephus Ilam. "What for?"

"Cheering us, of course," answered Carpentaria excitedly. "Isn't it immense?"

"Immense?" said Ilam heavily. "It's hot. What did you want to show me up here?"

"That!" exclaimed Carpentaria, pointing below to the City with a superb gesture. "And that!" he added passionately, pointing with another gesture to the whole of London, which lay spread out with all its towers and steeples and its blanket of smoke, tremendous and interminable to the east. "That is our prey," he said, "our food."

And he began to sing the Toreador song from "Carmen," exultantly launching the notes into the sky.

"Mr Carpentaria," said Josephus Ilam, with unexpected bitterness, "is this your idea of a joke? Bringing me up here to see London and our show, as if I didn't know London and our show like my pocket!"

Ilam's concealed hatred of Carpentaria, which had been slowly growing for more than a year, as a fire spreads secretly in the hold of a ship, seemed to spurt out a swift tongue of flame in the acrimony of his tone. Carpentaria was startled. Even then, in a sudden flash of illumination, he grasped to a certain extent the import of Ilam's attitude towards him, but he did not grasp it fully. How should he?

"Why," he said to himself, "I believe the old johnny dislikes me! What on earth for?" He could not understand all Ilam's reasons. "Pity!" he reflected further. "If the managers of a show like this can't hit it off together, there may be trouble."

In which supposition he was infinitely more right than he imagined.

He balanced himself lightly on the edge of the car, his left leg dangling, and seized one of the field-glasses which hung secured by thin steel chains round the inside of the wicker parapet, and putting it to his eyes, he gazed down at the Oriental Gardens. He must have seen something there that profoundly interested him, for the glasses remained glued to his eyes for a long time.

"I repeat," said Ilam firmly, standing up, "is this your idea of a joke?"

He was close to Carpentaria, and his glance was vicious.

"My friend," murmured, Carpentaria, dropping the glasses. "What's the matter with you is that you aren't an artist, not a bit of one. You are an excellent fellow, with a splendid head for figures, and I respect you enormously, but you haven't the artistic sense. If you had you would share the thrill which I feel as I survey our creation and that London over there. You would appreciate why I brought you up here."

"I'm a business man – a plain business man, that's what I am," said Ilam. "I've never pretended to be an artist, and I don't want to be an artist. Let me tell you that I ought to be in the advertisement department, and not canoodling my time away up here, Mr Carpentaria."

"My dear sir," said Carpentaria hastily, "accept my apologies. Let us descend at once."

"And while I'm about it," pursued Ilam unheedingly – his irritation was like a stone rolling down a hill – "while I'm about it, I'll point out that your objection to having advertisements on the walls of the restaurants is fatuous."

"But, my dear Ilam," Carpentaria protested, "people don't care to have to read advertisements while they're at their meals. It puts them off. For instance, to have it dinned into you that G. H. Mumm is the only champagne worth drinking when you happen to be drinking Heidsieck, or to have Wall's sausages thrust down your throat while you are toying with an ice-cream-people don't like it. We must think of our patrons. And, besides, it's so inarti -"

"Rubbish!" said Ilam. "One way and another these ads. would be worth a hundred a week to us."

"Well, and what's a hundred a week?"

"'It's the interest on a hundred and twenty thousand pounds," Ilam replied vivaciously. "And there's another thing. It would be much better if you employed more time in inspection instead of rehearsing and conducting your precious band. Any fool can

11

conduct a band. Give me a stick and I'd do it myself. But inspection-"

"My precious band!" stammered Carpentaria, aghast.

His very soul was laid low; and considering that Carpentaria's Band had been famous in the capitals of two continents for twelve years at least, it was not surprising that his soul should be laid low by this terrible phrase.

"Yes," said Ilam, "I've had enough of it." His shoulder touched Carpentaria's, and his eyes-little, like a pig's-shot arrows of light. "Supposing I shoved you over? I should have the concern to myself then, and no foolish interference."

He twisted his face into a grim laugh.

"You have a sense of humour, after all Ilam," responded gaily the man on the edge of the car, fingering his long red moustache, and he, too, laughed, but he got down from his perch.

"I'd just like you to comprehend-" Ilam began again.

But at that instant a head appeared above the edge of the central aperture of the car, and Ilam stopped.

It was the head of the young man in spectacles – gold-rimmed spectacles.

"I'm Smithers, of the *Morning Herald*," said the young man brightly and calmly, "and I took this opportunity of seeing you privately. Your men objected when I got into the parachute attachment, but you told 'em to let go, and so they let go. I've had some difficulty in climbing up here off the parachute bar. Dangerous rather. However, I've done it. I dare say you heard the crowd cheering."

"So it was him they were cheering," muttered Ilam, and then looked at Carpentaria.

Ilam was not a genius in the art of conversation. He could only say what he meant, and when the running of the City of Pleasure demanded the art of conversation he relied on Carpentaria, even if he was furious with him.

"What's the game?" asked Carpentaria.

"Well," said Smithers politely, "don't you think I deserve an interview?"

"You know we have absolutely declined all interviews."

"Yes, that's why the *Herald* wants one so badly; that's why I'm dangling a thousand feet above my grave."

Carpentaria and Ilam exchanged glances. Each read the thought of the other – that the spectacled Smithers might have overheard their conversation, and should therefore be handled with care, this side up. "Leave it to me," said the eyes of Carpentaria to the eyes of Ilam.

"Mr Smithers, of the *Herald* "-Carpentaria blossomed into the flowers of speech-" we heartily applaud your courage and your devotion to duty in a profession full of perils, but you are trespassing."

"Excuse me, I'm not," said Smithers. "You can only trespass on land and water, and this isn't a salmon river or a forbidden footpath. Besides, I've got my press season-ticket. Come now, talk to me."

"We are talking to you."

"I mean, answer my questions for the benefit of humanity. I'm the father of a family with two penniless aunts, and the *Herald* will probably sack me if I fail in this interview. Think of that."

"I prefer not to think of it," said Carpentaria. "However, we will answer any reasonable questions you care to put to us, on one condition."

"Name it," snapped Smithers.

"I will name it afterwards," said Carpentaria, looking at Ilam.

"All right," sighed Smithers, "I agree, whatever it is."

"You look like an honourable man. I shall trust you," Carpentaria remarked.

"Journalists are always honourable," said Smithers. "It is their employers who sometimes-however, that's neither here nor there. You may trust me. Now tell me. Why this objection to interviews? That's what's puzzling the public. You're a business concern, aren't you?"

"That's just the reason," said Carpentaria. "We aren't a star-actor or a bogus company. We're above interviews, we are. Do you catch Smith & Son, or Cook's, or the North-Western Railway, or Mrs Humphry Ward having themselves interviewed?"

"Not much," ejaculated Ilam glumly.

"People who refuse to be interviewed have a status that other people can never have. Our business is our business. When we want the public to know anything, we take a page in the *Herald*, say, and pay two hundred and fifty pounds for it, and inform the public exactly what we want 'em to know, in our own words. We do not require the assistance of interviewers. There's the whole secret. What next?"

"That seems pretty straight," Smithers agreed. "Another thing. Why have you gone and called this concern the City of Pleasure?"

"Because it is the City of Pleasure," growled Ilam.

"Yes, but it seems rather a fancy name, doesn't it? – rather too poetical, highfalutin?"

"That's merely because you journalists never have any imagination," Carpentaria explained. "You aren't used to this name yet. It was you journalists who cried out that the Crystal Palace was a too poetical and highfalutin name for that glass wigwam over there" – and he pointed to the twin towers of Sydenham in the distance – "but you've got used to it, and you admit now that it is the Crystal Palace and couldn't be anything else."

Smithers laughed.

"Good!" said he. "All that's nothing. Let me come to the core of the apple. Do you expect this thing to pay? Do you really mean it to pay, or is it only a millionaire's lark? You know all the experts are saying it can't pay."

"Can't it?" ejaculated Ilam.

"We shall take fifteen thousand pounds at the gates to-day," said Carpentaria. "The highest attendance in any one day at the Paris Exhibition of 1900 was six hundred thousand. Do you imagine we can't equal that? We shall surpass it, sir. Wait for our August fetes. Wait for our Congress of Trade Unions in September, and you will see! The average total attendance at the last three Paris exhibitions has been forty-five millions. We hope to reach fifty millions. But suppose we only reach forty millions. That means two million pounds in gates alone; and let me remind you that the minor activities of this show are self-supporting. Why, the Chicago Exhibition made a profit of nearly a million and a half dollars. Do you suppose we can't beat that, with a city of six million people at our doors, and the millions of Lancashire and Yorkshire within four hours of us?"

"But Chicago was State-aided," Mr Smithers ventured.

"State-aided!" cried Ilam. "Chicago was the worst-managed show in the history of shows, except St. Louis. If the State came to me I should – I should

"Offer it a penny to go away and play in the next : Street." Carpentaria finished his sentence for him.

"You interest me extremely," said the journalist. "And now, as to the number of your employees."

He chuckled to himself with glee at the splendid 'interview he was getting out of Carpentaria and Ilam as they obligingly responded to his queries. It was Ilam who at last revolted, and insisted that he must descend.

"Now for my condition," said Carpentaria.

"Let's have it," said the journalist.

"You asked us to talk to you and we have talked to you. The condition is that you regard all you have heard up here as strictly confidential – mind, all! You tell no one; you print nothing. Remember, you are an honourable man."

"But this is farcical," Smithers expostulated.

"Not at all," said Carpentaria sweetly. "Do you imagine that because you have an inordinate amount of cheek, a family and two penniless aunts, we are going to break the habits of a lifetime? For myself, I have never been interviewed."

"Is this your last word?" the journalist demanded.

"It is," said Carpentaria.

"Very well," said the journalist, and his head disappeared.

"Let us descend," said Ilam, savagely pleased. And he waved the descent flag.

"We shan't descend just yet," the journalist informed them, popping up his head again.

"And pray, why not?"

"Because I've cut the rope."

Carpentaria, always calm when art was not concerned, tore a fragment of paper from an envelope in his pocket and threw it out of the car. It sank away rapidly from the balloon. Moreover, it was evident, even to the eye, that their distance from the earth was vastly increasing.

"I withdraw my promise now this moment," said the journalist, climbing carefully into the car. "Everything that you say henceforward will be printed. We shall have quite an exciting trip. We may even get to France. Anyhow, I shall have a clinking column for Monday's *Herald*. You evidently hadn't quite appreciated what the new journalism is."

Then there was silence in the mounting balloon.

Ilam bent his malevolent eyes longingly upon the disappearing scene below. The glory of the sunshine was nothing to him. He wanted to be in the advertisement department, arranging future contracts for spaces on the programmes. He reflected that it was another of the mad caprices of Carpentaria that had got him into this grotesque scrape. And he was so angry that he forgot even to think of the danger to which he was exposed.

"So here we are!" said the journalist. "And you can't do anything!"

3

INSPIRATION

"Permit me to say, Mr Smithers," Carpentaria remarked at last, "that your knavery is futile. The resources of civilisation are not yet exhausted. We are, in fact, already descending."

He held tightly in his hand the end of a rope, which reached up high above them and was lost in the mass of cordage. He had opened the valve to its widest.

"Don't venture to move," he added, "or Mr Ilam will break your head for you. This affair will cost us nothing but a few thousand cubic feet of gas at half-a-crown a thousand. What it will cost you, I shall have to consider."

And without saying anything further for the moment, he unloosed a very thin cable that was wound round a windlass in the car itself, and, tying a white flag at the end of it, he began to lower it rapidly over the edge of the car.

Thanks to the perfect calm which reigned, the balloon was still well over the Amusements Park.

Soon the voyagers could perceive the excited movements of the crowds below, and then the white flag touched earth, and was seized by the eager hands of the balloonists, and slowly the balloon, in a condition bordering on collapse, subsided to the ground with the gentleness of a fatigued British workman falling asleep. And great cheers, for the second time that day, filled the air.

"You might have been sure," said Carpentaria, when they were ten feet off safety, "that in a show like this due precautions would be taken against accidents and idiots!"

Smithers, nearly as limp as the balloon, made no reply. Josephus Ilam glared over him.

"It's nothing, it's nothing!" cried Carpentaria to the staff, who besieged the party with questions. "Fill her up as quick as you can, attach the rope and get ready for your public. Don't bother me!"

And he leapt out of the car and was running, literally running, away, when Ilam called out:

"Hi! wait a minute. What's to be done with this maniac here?" And Ilam muttered to himself, "Why does he run away like that? What's his next caprice going to be?"

"I was forgetting," said Carpentaria, stopping. "Young man" – and he addressed Smithers severely – "follow me, and no nonsense!"

Smithers obediently followed, pushing after Carpentaria through the curious crowds. They came at length to the Central Way, and Carpentaria halted and took Smithers by the coat collar.

"Listen!" said he. "We're much too busy to trouble with police-court proceedings. And, besides, there's your brace of penniless aunts. Cut! Clear out! Hook it! I rather admire you. See?"

Smithers saw, and vanished.

Carpentaria hastened on, rushing across the Central Way, scarcely avoiding cable-cars, and so, by a private passage between two shops, into the Oriental Gardens. Now, just within the Oriental Gardens, on either side of the grand entrance to them, were two spacious houses, built in the bungalow style, with enclosed gardens of their own. One of these was occupied by Josephus Ilam and his mother, and the other by Carpentaria and his half-sister, Juliette D'Avray. Between the house of Ilam and the back of the shops in Central Way was one of those small waste trifles of ground which often get left in planning a vast exhibition or show. It was skilfully hidden from the view of the public by wooden palisades, and in this palisading was a door, painted so as to escape detection. The plot of ground, about three yards by two, was already being utilised for lumber. Carpentaria entered by the door and shut it after him. A man – a middle-aged man, in a blue suit of rather shabby appearance – was seated on some planks. He started up, and then seemed to sway.

"What are you doing here?" Carpentaria curtly demanded.

"Look 'ere," said the man, swaying towards Carpentaria, "I'm aw ri' – you're aw ii' – eh? I'm a gemman. Come here to res' – rest. You leave me 'lone – I leave you 'lone. Stop, I give you my car'."

The man was obviously inebriated, and Carpentaria was in no mood to spend precious minutes in diplomacy with a victim of Bacchus. He departed, shutting the door, and leaving the victim fumbling with a card-case. He meant to send some one to eject the man, but he forgot.

"Say!" cried the drunkard after him, "how ju know I wazz 'ere? Mus' been up in a b'loon – I repea' – b'loon."

In another moment Carpentaria was in the study of his bungalow, panting.

"Quick!" he said to Juliette, an extremely natty little woman of thirty or so.

He sank into the chair before his desk. Juliette placed some music-paper in front of him and put a pen in his hand, and he scrawled across the top of the page "The Balloon Lullaby," and began to scribble notes – quavers, crotchets, semibreves, and some other strange wonders – all over the page.

"It came to me all of a sudden," he murmured, "while we were up in the balloon."

"Don't talk, dear," said Juliette. "Write."

And he wrote.

When it was finished Carpentaria wiped his brow and drank a whisky and milk which Juliette had prepared for him. He sighed with content and exhaustion. The creative crisis was over.

"Play it," he ejaculated.

And Juliette sat down at the piano near the window overlooking the magnificent gardens, and played softly the two hundred and forty-seventh opus of Carpentaria.

"It is lovely," she said.

"Yes," he admitted. "It's a classy little thing. Came to me just like that!" He snapped his fingers.

"Your best ones always do," Juliette smiled.

"I'll have that performed this very night," he stated.

4

MRS ILAM

Somewhat later on the same afternoon, in the drawing-room of the house opposite, Josephus Ilam was drinking tea with his mother. The aged Mrs Ilam, who was very thin and not in the least tall – her son would have made a dozen of her – sat tremendously upright in her chair, while Josephus lolled his great bulk in angry attitudes on a sofa, near which the tea-table had been placed. Mrs Ilam wore widow's weeds, though it was many years since she had lost her husband, a man who had made a vast fortune out of soda-water – in the days when soda-water *was* soda-water. She had a narrow, hard face, with intensely black eyes, and intensely white hair, and when she directed those eyes upon her son, it became instantly plain that her son was at once her idol and her slave. She lived solely for this man of fifty, who had scarcely ever left her side. For her this mass of fifteen stone four was still a young child, needing watchful care and constant advice. Certainly she spoilt him; but, just as certainly, he went in awe of her. The fact that by judicious investments in hotel and public-house property he had more than doubled the fortune which his father left, did not at all improve his standing with the antique dame; it only made him in her view a clever boy with financial leanings. Moreover, every penny of the Ilam fortune was legally hers during her lifetime. Even Ilam's share in the City of Pleasure was hers. When

21

Carpentaria had discovered him, he had had to decide whether or not he should put more than a million pounds into the enterprise, and it was his mother who decided, who listened to everything, and then briefly told him that he would be a fool to leave the thing alone.

"Well," she said, in her high quavering voice, as she passed him a cup of tea – the cup rattled on the saucer in her blue-veined parchment hand – "so you are not getting on with Carpentaria? I was afraid you wouldn't."

"He won't listen to reason about the advertisements," said Ilam crossly, stirring his tea.

"No?"

"And he's absolutely mad about his music. He's spent ten hours in rehearsing this last two days. All the work I've had to do myself."

"Indeed!"

"And then, to crown his exploits, he takes me up in the balloon, mother – wastes a solid hour."

"In the balloon!"

Ilam recounted the incident of the balloon.

"And, after all, he lets that impudent journalist go free – absolutely free!"

"Jos," said his mother, "it's a wonder you're alive, my dear."

"It's a pity Carpentaria's alive," rejoined Ilam.

His mother's burning eyes met his.

"That's just what I've been thinking," she piped calmly.

Her son's gaze dropped.

"Since when?"

"Since you began grumbling about him, last week but one, my pet."

"He's no use now," Ilam grumbled. "We've carried out all his ideas, and it's simply a matter of business, and Carpentaria doesn't know the meaning of the word 'business.' Just think of his argument about those ads.!"

"Never mind that, Jos," Mrs Ilam put in.

"He's only in the way now," Jos proceeded gloomily.

"I suppose he wouldn't retire," Mrs Ilam suggested.

"Retire? Of course he wouldn't retire – nothing would induce him to retire. He enjoys it – he enjoys annoying me."

"Anyway," said the mother, "you'll have the satisfaction of a very great success."

She looked out of the window at the gardens.

"Yes," growled Ilam. "And he gets half the profits. I've found all the money, and he hasn't found a cent. But he gets half the profits. What for? A few ideas – nothing else. He pretends to direct, but he'll direct nothing except his blessed band. And I reckon we shall clear a profit of ten thousand a week! Half of ten is five."

"He only gets half the profits as long as he lives, Jos," said Mrs Ilam. "After that – nothing."

"Nothing," agreed Jos, biting cruelly into a hot scone. "But as long as he lives he's costing me, say, five thousand a week, besides worry."

"He mayn't live long," Mrs Ilam ventured.

"No, but he may live fifty years."

"Supposing he died very suddenly, Jos," Mrs Ilam pursued calmly; "he wouldn't be the first person that was inconvenient to you who had disappeared unexpectedly."

"Mother!" Ilam almost shouted, starting up.

"But would he?" Mrs Ilam persisted.

"No, he wouldn't," muttered Josephus, and his voice trembled.

Mrs Ilam blew out the spirit-lamp under the kettle as though she was blowing out Carpentaria.

"I'm off," said Josephus nervously.

"Wait a moment, child. Ring the bell for me."

A servant entered.

"Bring me your master's knitted waistcoat," said Mrs Ilam.

"But mother, I shan't want it."

"Yes, you will, Jos. There's no month more treacherous than May. You'll put it on to please me."

He obeyed, bent down to kiss his terrible parent, and departed.

"Think it over," she called out after him.

Ilam stopped.

"And then, what about his sister?" he said.

"Don't mix up two quite separate things," Mrs Ilam responded. "Besides, she isn't his sister."

5

THE BAND

That night the City of Pleasure was illuminated. Eighty thousand tiny electric lamps hanging in festoons from standard to standard lighted the Central Way alone; the facades of all the places of amusement were outlined in fire; the shops glittered; and the cable-cars, as they flashed to and fro, bore the mono-gram I.C. in electricity on their foreheads. At eight o'clock the thoroughfare was crowded with visitors, and the stream of arrivals was stronger than ever. In the superb restaurants, at all prices (no matter what the price, they were equally superb in decoration), five thousand diners were finishing five thousand dinners, their eyes undisturbed by the presence of advertisements on the walls. The theatre, the music-hall, the circus, the menagerie, the concerts, and the rest of the entertainments, were filling up. In the Amusements Park people shot down railways into water, slid down smooth slopes into mattresses, circled in great wheels, floated in the latest novelties of merry-go-rounds, ascended in the balloon, and practised all the other devices for frittering away eternity, just as though night had not fallen. In the vast court of the Exposition Palace a band was swelling the strains of the newest waltzes to three storeys of loungers and sitters at cafe-tables, while within the interior of the building men and women wandered about examining the multifarious attractions of the Woman's Exhibition.

But the chief joy was the Oriental Gardens, wherein a multitude of over fifty thousand persons had gathered together. The Oriental Gardens were illuminated, but in a different manner from the Central Way. Chinese lanterns were suspended everywhere in the budding trees, giving the illusion of magic precocious flowers that had blossomed there in a single hour, in all the tints of the rainbow and many others entirely foreign to the rainbow. The bandstand alone was picked out in electricity. It blazed in the centre of the gardens like a giant's crown, and, although yet empty, it formed the main object of attention. Overhead stretched a dark-blue sky, silvered with stars, and the wind had a warm and caressing quality which encouraged sightseers to expose themselves to it to such an extent that the fifteen cafes of the Oriental Gardens, some sheltered, some quite open, but each a centre of light and laughter, were every one crowded with guests. The four thousand chairs surrounding the bandstand were occupied, and also the six thousand other chairs dispersed in various parts of the gardens. The murmur of conversation, the rustle of dresses, the tinkle of glasses, the rumour of uncountable footsteps, rose on the air. The faces of pretty women could be observed obscurely in the delicious gloom, and the glowing scarlet of cigars bobbed mysteriously about like a species of restless glow-worm.

And everybody was conscious of the sensation of the extraordinary and amazing success of the great show. The evening papers had carried the news of the wonderful thing to each suburb of London. These papers gave from hour to hour the number of the persons who had passed the turnstiles, and calculated the number of tons of shillings that Ilam and Carpentaria would have to bank on Monday morning. But the principal thing that struck the evening papers was the complete readiness of the City of Pleasure. No detail of it was unfinished, and all agreed that this phenomenon stood unique in the history of the art of amusing immense crowds. All felt that a new era of amusement enterprise had been ushered in by Ilam and

Carpentaria, that everything was changed, and that in the future an enlightened and excessively exacting public would not be satisfied with what had pleased it in the past. And the owners of old-fashioned resorts trembled in their shoes, and hated Ilam and Carpentaria, while the myriad patrons of Ilam and Carpentaria on that first day flattered themselves that they had personally assisted at the birth of the grand innovation, and thought how they would say to their grandchildren: "Yes, I was present at the opening of the City of Pleasure, and a marvellous affair it was," and so on, in the manner of grandparents.

All were expecting Carpentaria, the lion of the show.

His band was due to perform from eight o'clock to ten, and special bills, posted on the sides of the gilded bandstand and in the cafes, announced: "Carpentaria's band will play the Balloon Lullaby, the latest composition of Carpentaria, composed this afternoon."

At ten minutes before eight the members of the band, sixty in number, and clad in the imperial purple uniform, marched in Indian file across the gardens to the stand. At a distance of ten paces from the end of the procession came Carpentaria, preceded by a small page bearing his baton on a cushion of purple velvet. Carpentaria always did things with overwhelming style and solemnity. Superior persons laughed at the style and solemnity, but the vast majority did not laugh; they cheered; they appreciated. Whether they were right or wrong, the indubitable fact is, that these things came naturally to Carpentaria; they were the expression of his exceedingly theatrical soul, the devices of a man who believes in himself.

At eight o'clock precisely Carpentaria faced the fifty thousand from his bandstand, and, after having bowed elaborately thrice, turned to the band, and lifted the sacred stick.

It was a dramatic moment, the real inauguration of the City of Pleasure.

Cheers and hurrahs rolled in terrific volumes of sound across the gardens, and they did not cease; and people not acquainted with the fame and renown of Carpentaria perceived what it was to be a favourite of capitals, a leading star in the galaxy of stars that the public salutes and recognises.

Carpentaria preserved the immobility of carven stone until the plaudits had ceased; they lasted for exactly five and a half minutes. Consequently the concert was exactly five and half minutes late in commencing. Carpentaria himself was never late, but his public had a habit of delaying him.

Suddenly he brought down his Baton with a surprising shock. The carven stone had started into life, and "God save the King" was under way.

Now to see Carpentaria conduct was one of the sights of the world. He conducted not merely with his hand and eye, but with the whole of his immortal frame, and his uniform. It was said that he was capable of conducting the Eroica Symphony of Beethoven with his left foot – and who shall deny it? "God save the King" was child's play to him. Moreover, he showed a certain reserve in handling it. He merely conducted it as though in conducting it he himself were literally saving the King. That was all. But with what snap, what dash, what chic, what splash and what magnificent presence of mind did he save the King! The applause was wild and ample.

The next item was "The City of Pleasure March," composed by Carpentaria. Indeed, Carpentaria conducted nothing but national hymns, his own compositions, and, as a superlative concession, Wagner and Beethoven. "The City of Pleasure" was in Carpentaria's finest style, and it was planned to give him the fullest scope in conducting it. He had already made it famous in a triumphal tour through the United States in the previous year. It began with the utmost possible volume of sound. It had a contagious and infectious lilt to it, and both the lilt and the volume of sound were continued without the slightest respite during the whole composition. In the course of this masterpiece Carpentaria performed physical feats that would have astounded Cinquevalli and the Schaffer Troupe. In the frenzy of self-expression he all but stood on his head. The bandstand was too small for him; he needed a planet on which to circulate. By turns his baton was a sceptre, a pump-handle, a maypole, a crutch, a drumstick, a flag, a toothpick, a mop, a pendulum, a whip, a bottle of soothing-syrup, and a scorpion. By turns he whipped, tortured, encouraged, liberated, imprisoned, mopped up, measured, governed, diverted, pushed over, pulled back, and turned inside out his band, and whenever their enthusiasm seemed likely to lead them into indiscretions, he soothed them with the soothing-syrup. By turns the conducting of the piece was a march, a campaign, a house on fire, the race for the Derby, the forging of a hundred-ton gun, a display of fireworks, a mayoral banquet, and a mother scolding a numerous family.

It was colossal.

At the close, as sudden as the shutting of a door, there was a vast strange silence, and then the applause as colossal as the piece, broke out like a conflagration.

Carpentaria bowed; the entire band bowed; Carpentaria bowed again. Lastly he indicated a flute-player with his baton, and the flute-player came forward and shared the glory of Carpentaria. Why a flute-player, no one could have guessed. Forty flutes could not have been heard in that terrific concourse of brass and drums. But Carpentaria was Carpentaria.

"Did any of you hear the sound of a shot?" Carpentaria said in a low voice to his band.

"Shot? No, sir," came from a dozen mouths. "Why, sir?"

"Because a bullet has just grazed my ear. It was in the fourth bar from the end." He put his hand to his ear and showed blood on his finger. "It's nothing, nothing," he quietened them. "I shall expect you to behave as though nothing had occurred, as soldiers in fact."

"Certainly, sir," replied the intrepid band.

Carpentaria gazed at one of the iron supports of the roof of the bandstand. In a line with his head the surface of the pillar had been damaged and dented. He disturbed two trombone-players in order to search the floor, and in a few seconds he had found a flattened bullet, which he put in his pocket.

"Number two," he said sharply, going to his desk and tapping it.

Number two was the lullaby. No more striking contrast to the march could have been found. It was so delicate, so softly stealing, that you could scarcely hear it; and yet you could hear it – you could hear it everywhere. Carpentaria drew sweetness out of his band with the gestures of a conjurer drawing an interminable roll of coloured paper from his mouth, previously shown to be empty. It was the daintiest thing, swaying in the air like gossamer. It brought tears to the orbs of mothers, and made strong men close their eyes. Such was the versatility of Carpentaria.

The applause amounted to a furore.

"I give you my word of honour, ladies and gentlemen," said Carpentaria, coming to the rail of the stand and stilling the cheers with a gesture, "at half-past three this afternoon not a note of the little piece was composed."

His demeanour gave no sign of agitation. But at the close of the concert, no more bullets having arrived, he wiped his brow with relief. Most of the band did the same.

He walked about on the river terrace for over an hour, calming his spirit, which had been through so many excitements, artistic and otherwise, during the afternoon and evening. And he meditated, now on the bullet, and now on Ilam. He could scarcely realise how nearly he had escaped quarrelling with Ilam in the balloon; their relations hitherto had been invariably amicable, at any rate on the surface; and he had done so much for Ilam; he had put a second fortune in Ilam's pocket. The dazzling success of the day of inauguration was the success of Carpentaria's ideas. And yet Ilam hated him. He felt that Ilam hated him. He almost shuddered as he remembered the moment when he had sat on the dizzy edge of the balloon-car, and Ilam had threatened him, and then laughed.

The Oriental Gardens were empty and dark. The gay crowd had departed; the lights were extinguished. Only the light in Ilam's drawing-room shone across the expanse as it had shone through all the evening. Carpentaria's own bungalow was dark. He wondered what Juliette was doing.

At length he set off home through the gardens. And just as he was entering his front door he recollected that he had given no instructions about the drunken man in the enclosure. He turned back down the steps, and went into the enclosure and struck a match. The man was lying on the ground, no doubt asleep.

"Well, this is a caution!" he muttered.

A notion occurred to him, one of his fanciful pranks. He picked up the unconscious man, who held himself stiff and did not even groan, and carried him, not with too much difficulty – for Carpentaria was extremely powerful – to the side-door-of Ilam's residence; he placed the form against the door. Every night for weeks past Ilam had come out by that door about midnight to take a final stroll of inspection. He felt that he owed Ilam a grudge. Then he retired into the shadow and waited.

Presently the door opened, and Ilam fell over the man, as Carpentaria hoped he would, and picked himself up with oaths and struck a match and gazed at the form.

At the same instant a woman's figure passed Carpentaria in the dark. He was surprised to recognise Juliette. He touched her.

"Oh!" she cried softly, starting back.

"Why do you start like that?" he demanded.

"You – you – frightened me," she said.

He escorted her into their house. When he came out again Ilam was descending the steps by the side-door. Nothing lay near the door.

"Seen anything of a drunken man?" Carpentaria called out.

"No," said Ilam, after a pause.

"Not near your door?"

"No. Why?"

"Oh, nothing. Only I thought I saw one."

"Good night," growled Ilam, but instead of taking the air he returned abruptly to the house.

6

The Black Burden

"Curious!" Carpentaria meditated as he retired to his abode. "Having fallen over a man lying drunk on his steps, why should my friend and partner, Mr Josephusllam, totally deny that he has seen a drunken man? With my own eyes I saw him tumble. Now this mishap must have made Mr Josephus Ilam angry, because he is just the sort of person who does get angry upon the provocation of a pure accident. Yet, so far as I could judge in the gloom, there was no trace of anger in his demeanour when he answered my question. On the contrary, he appeared to be rather subdued.

"And further – what has become of my friend the drunken man? The drunken man must exist somewhere. Is he in Ilam's house? And, if so, why is he in Ilam's house? Neither Josephus nor his mother is precisely a type of the Good Samaritan. And if he is not in Ilam's house, has he suddenly recovered and walked away on his legs unaided? Impossible! I was once drunk, and I say, impossible. Then, has Josephus carried him somewhere? And where has he carried him, and why?"

Carpentaria unlocked his front-door and entered the hall of his dwelling, and then-locked and bolted the door. He was not in the habit of either locking or bolting his front-door; the idea of so securing a house which stood in the middle of half a square mile of private property, well guarded at all its gates, seemed ridiculous. Nevertheless he did it, and he could have given no reason for doing it. He imagined that he heard footsteps in the passage leading from the hall to the kitchen, and he quickly turned on the electric light and looked down the passage. But there was nothing. He decided that he was very nervous and impressionable that night. The servants had, doubtless, long since gone to bed. He extinguished the light and made his way upstairs to his study, and sat down in his chair – the famous chair in which he composed his famous melodies. The faint illumination of the May night made the principal objects in the room vaguely visible. He could discern the pale square of the framed autograph letter from President McKinley which hung on the opposite wall. He tried to collect his ideas and think in a logical sequence.

Then, again, he fancied that he heard footsteps, and that he saw a dim form near the door.

"Who's that?" he cried sharply.

"It's only me," answered a woman's voice, and the electricity was at the same instant switched on.

Juliette stood there.

"Why are you sitting in the dark, Carlos?" she demanded.

Carlos was her pet name for him.

"I don't know," he said lamely.

"My poor dear," she smiled, approaching him. "I haven't said good night to you."

She put her long and elegant hands on his shoulders, as was her wont each evening, and kissed him on both cheeks in her French fashion. The affection between Carlos and his half-French half-sister was real and profound. He liked her for her Parisian daintiness, and for the eminently practical qualities which she possessed in common with most French women, and also because she regarded him as a genius. To-night he thought she was sweeter and more sisterly than ever.

"Good night," she said, and her voice trembled, and a slight humidity glistened in her eyes.

"Good night," he responded.

And she tripped off, swinging the perfect skirt of her black *mousseline* dress round the edge of the door.

"She's mightily excited to-night," he murmured to himself; and he reflected, as all men reflect from time to time, that women are strange and incomprehensible, a device invented by Providence to keep the wit of man well sharpened by constant employment.

He passed into his bedroom, and went out on to the wooden balcony of the bedroom, which commanded a view of Ilam's side-door. A light showed through the glass above the door, and Carpentaria noticed at length that the door was slightly ajar. He stepped back into the bedroom, extinguished all his own lights, and returned to the balcony to watch. He determined to watch as long as Ilam's door remained ajar. He sat down in a cane chair provided for repose on the balcony, and his one regret was that the glow of a cigarette or a cigar would betray him.

He grew calmer. The frenzy into which music always threw him had quite worn itself away. He was able to think clearly. He did not, however, think so much upon the incident of the drunken man "as upon the incident of the bullet; and this was perhaps natural. He was astounded now that he could have remained in the bandstand, so utterly careless of danger, after the arrival of the bullet. He was astounded, too, at the sang-froid of his musicians. But, then, their ears had not been grazed, and his had. He saw that he was at the mercy of any homicidal maniac who, on a dark night, with a good rifle and a sure aim, chose to secrete himself in some deserted alley of the vast Oriental Gardens, and shoot at him during a loud burst of music. And he said: "Well, if I am to die, I am to die, and there's an end of it. Assuming that a given man A has really determined to kill another given man B, and A is obstinate, nothing will ultimately save B. I am B. Hence I must be philosophical."

But who was A?

He thought of all the enemies he had made, all the rivals he had defeated, but the process of their enumeration was perfunctory. For out of the depths of his mind rose persistently one name, again, and again, and again, and yet again, like a succession of bubbles, all alike, rising to the surface of a pond and breaking there. And that name was the name of Ilam. He forbade the name to rise, but it rose. With the simplicity which marked some of his mental processes, he could not understand why Ilam should hate him murderously. But the episode of the balloon had magically and terribly cast a new and searching light on the recesses of Ilam's character. He felt that hitherto he had been mistaken in Ilam, and that Ilam was not a person with whom it was wise to have interests in common. And the unknown designs of Ilam seemed to surround him in the night like the web of a gigantic spider, and to bind him tighter and tighter.

Then his reflections were interrupted by a sound somewhere below the balcony.

It was the sound of his own side-door being very cautiously opened. He could hear it perfectly clearly in the still night; but whether the door was being opened from the outside or the inside he could not tell. He remembered that, though he had bolted and locked the front-door, he had utterly forgotten the side-door. He leaned over the balcony as far as he dared, but even so he could catch ho glimpse of anything in the obscurity beneath.

And then there were steps on the gravel, and he saw a white blur moving on the top of a dark mass. In another moment he perceived that the apparition was Juliette, with a white shawl wrapped round her head. What was she doing there, and why had she opened the door so cautiously? Had she some secret? He decided to watch her. She moved to the middle of the avenue between the two houses and hesitated. And then the great clock in the tower of the Exposition Palace tolled the hour of twelve solemnly, as it were warningly, over the immense extent of the sleeping City of Pleasure.

The appeal of the clock seemed to Carpentaria to be almost dramatic. He felt strongly that he could not spy upon Juliette, that he could not be disloyal to this affectionate companion of his life, and honourably he called out to her:

"Juliette, what are you doing?"

His own voice startled him. It was so clear and penetrative in the gloom.

There was a slight pause. Then Juliette replied:

"Carlos, you seem bent on frightening me to-night. I thought you were in bed and asleep. You'll take cold on that balcony. I only came out to get a little air."

The notion struck him that her head was turned directly to Ilam's house, and yet she made no comment on the light there and the door ajar.

"Go in, there's a good girl," said Carpentaria. "It's you who'll be taking cold."

"I'm going in," she answered.

And she went in.

He had yet another alarm. Something moved on the balcony itself, near a row of flower-pots. Then he felt a pressure against his leg.

"Ah, Beppo!" he whispered, suddenly relieved, smiling at his nervous timidity. A great Angora cat leaped on to his knees, and began clawing at the superb pile of his purple trousers. He stroked the animal, and Beppo purred with a volume of sound equal to that of many sawmills. "Don't purr so loud, Bep," he advised the cat; but the cat, under the impression that it was the centre of importance in the best of all possible worlds, purred with undiminished vigour.

Five minutes, ten minutes, a quarter of an hour passed so, and then Carpentaria heard heavy footsteps in the avenue from the direction of the Central Way. He jumped up, shattering the illusions of Beppo, and listened intently. A man presently appeared, walking slowly. He wondered who it could be; but when the figure paused at Ilam's steps, mounted them, and pushed open the unlatched door, he saw that it was Ilam himself, and that Ilam was holding in his arms a bundle of what looked like black cloth. The vision of him was but transient, for Ilam closed the door at once. Ilam, then, must have left his house before Carpentaria had come on to the balcony. The watcher on the balcony felt his heart beating rapidly. His calm had vanished. The frenzy of the music, the perturbation caused by the bullet, had passed, only to give way to another and perhaps a more dreadful excitation. What could these secret journeys of Ilam portend? He clutched fiercely the rail of the balcony in his apprehensive anxiety.

After a time – not a very long time – the door opened again, and for at least five seconds Josephus Ilam stood plainly silhouetted against a light within the house, and over his shoulders, which were bent, he carried an enormous limp burden, draped in black. He looked back into the house once, then turned awkwardly, because of his burden, to shut the door behind him, and with excessive deliberation descended the steps and came out into the avenue. The figure and its burden were now nothing but a shape in the gloom.

Carpentaria decided in the fraction of a second what he would do. He slipped into his bedroom, took off his boots, put on a pair of felt slippers, scurried downstairs, opened the side-door, and gently slipped out. Ilam, tramping slowly with clumsy footsteps, had reached the arch leading to the Central Way.

7

THE CAT

Carpentaria dogged him with all the precautions of silence as he turned to the right down the Central Way. The great thoroughfare of the City of Pleasure was, of course, absolutely deserted. Its fountains were stilled; its pretty cable-cars had disappeared; its flags had been hauled down. The meagre trees rustled chilly in the night-wind. Its vast and floriated white architecture seemed under the sombre sky to be the architecture of a dream. The one sign of human things was the illuminated face of the clock over the Exposition Palace, which showed twenty-five minutes past twelve. Of the two thousand souls employed in the City, more than half had gone to their homes in the other city, London, and several hundreds slept in the dormitories that had been built for them at the southern extremity of the Central Way. The remaining hundred or so were dispersed in various parts of the City, either watching or asleep. Some had the right to sleep at their posts. But the men of the highly organised fire service would be awake and alert.

Yet there happened to be no living creature on the Way, except its two chiefs. Ilam crossed the Way, and turned off it through an avenue that lay between the lecture hall and the menagerie. Carpentaria followed at a safe distance, hiding in the thick shadows as he went. From the interior of the menagerie came the subdued growls and groans of the wild beasts therein,

39

suffering from insomnia, and longing for the jungle. Among the treasures of the menagerie was a society of twenty-seven lions, who went through a performance twice a day under their trainer, Brant, the king of lion-tamers, as he was called on the City of Pleasure programmes, and as he, in fact, was. There were also a celebrated sanguinary tiger, that had killed three men in New York, and various other delicate attractions. The nocturnal noises of these fearsome animals were sufficiently appalling. And when Ilam stopped before a little door in the south facade of the menagerie building, a cold perspiration froze the forehead and the spirit of Carpentaria. Was the man going to yield his mysterious black-enveloped burden to the lions and the tigers, the jackals and the hyenas, of that inestimable collection of African and Asiatic fauna?

But Ilam struggled onwards. And next they passed the electricity works, which was in full activity, for the manufacture of light went on night and day in the City of Pleasure. Ilam slunk along the front of the workshops, increasing his pace. Fortunately for him, the windows were seven feet from the ground, so that he could not be observed from within. The whirr of the wheels revolving incessantly in front of gigantic magnets filled the air, and from the high windows shone a steely-blue radiance, chequered by the flying shadows of machinery.

Ilam turned again, and entered the Amusements Park, and, threading his way among chutes, switchbacks, slides, and ponds, he crossed it from end to end.

"Where is he going?" Carpentaria muttered.

And then, suddenly, it occurred to Carpentaria where Ilam was going.

Behind the Amusements Park, and abutting on the confines of the City territory, was a large waste piece of ground which had been used for excavations and for refuse. In the tremendous operation of levelling the site of the City, digging foundations, and gardening in the landscape manner, much earth had been needed in one spot, and much earth had had to be removed in another. The waste piece of ground was the clearing-house of this business. In certain parts it was humped like a camel's back, and in others it was hollowed into pits. Immense quantities of soil lay loose, and there were, besides, barrows and spades in abundance.

Arrived in the midst of this sterile wilderness, Ilam, unceremoniously dropped his burden near a miniature mountain, which raised itself by the side of a miniature pit. He then found a spade, and, having tested the looseness of the soil, took up the black mystery and slipped it carefully into the pit. Then he climbed with the spade on to the summit of the hillock, and began to push the soil from the hillock into the pit. It proved to be the simplest thing in the world. In five minutes the burden lay under several feet of soil.

Carpentaria, favoured by the nature of the spot, had crept closer.

"Earth to earth, ashes to ashes, dust to dust!" he heard Ilam reciting. Amazing phenomenon! But nothing can be more amazing than the behaviour of an utterly respectable man when he is committing a crime!

The affair finished, Ilam departed, passing within a few feet of Carpentaria, who stretched himself flat on the ground to avoid detection.

And when Ilam had vanished out of sight, Carpentaria jumped up feverishly, seized the spade, leapt into the pit, and began to dig – to dig with a fury of haste. Fate helped him, for the black mass was uncovered in less time than had been taken to cover it. He dragged it slowly out of the pit, and slowly, almost reluctantly, unwrapped it. He had been sure at the first touch that it was the body of a man, and he was not mistaken. In the gloomy night he could see the white patches made by the face and the hands. The body was not yet stiff. He hesitated, and then struck a match. He hoped the wind would blow it out, but the wind spared it; it flared bravely, and lighted the face of the corpse, and the corpse was that of the mysterious drunken man.

A thousand unanswerable questions fought together for solution in Carpentaria's brain.

He knew himself to be in the presence of a crime, of a murder. His legal duty, therefore, was to fetch justice in the shape of a policeman. But he reflected that no battalion of policemen and judges could undo the crime, bring the dead to life, make innocent the guilty. He reflected also upon the clumsiness of State justice, and the inconveniences attaching to it, and upon the immeasurable harm its advent might do to the opening season of the City of Pleasure. Moreover, he had a horror of capital punishment, and he was a bold and original man, though an artist. He settled rapidly in his mind that he himself would probe the matter to its root, and that the justice involved should be the private justice of Carpentaria, not the public justice of the realm.

And a few minutes later he had discovered a long, flat barrow, and was wheeling away the burden that had bent the back of Josephus Ilam. He brought it circuitously and gently by way of the Sports Fields round again to the Central Way, and so to the neighbourhood of his own house. The night had now grown darker that ever, and a few drops of rain began to fall.

Suddenly, as he was approaching the two bungalows, he stopped and listened. He thought he heard footsteps; but no sound met his ear, and he raised the handles of the barrow again. By this time he was midway between the bungalows and about to turn to the side-entrance of his own. Once more he stopped; he distinctly did hear footsteps crushing the gravel.

"What is that? Any one there?" cried a voice.

And it was Ilam's voice, full of fear. Carpentaria crept away to the shelter of his own wall, leaving the barrow that had become a bier in the midst of the path. Vaguely and dimly he saw the form of Ilam coming down the avenue, saw it stop uncertainly before the barrow, saw it bend down, and then he heard a shriek – a shriek of terror – loud, violent, and echoing, and Ilam fled away. Carpentaria heard him mount the steps of his house and fumble with the door, and then he heard the bang of the door.

With all possible speed he rushed to the barrow, wheeled it into his garden, and thence to an outhouse, of which he carefully fastened the padlock.

He stood some time hesitant in the avenue, wondering whether any further phenomenon would proceed from the Ilam house that night. His curiosity was rewarded. A most strange procession emerged presently from the bungalow. First came old Mrs Ilam, dressed in a crimson dressing-gown, a white nightcap on her head, and carrying a lamp with an elaborate drawing-room shade. Carpentaria could see that the lamp shook in her trembling hand. Her hands always trembled, but her head never. She came down the steps with the deliberation of extreme old age, peering in front of her, and she was followed, timorously, by her son. The lamp threw a large circle of yellow light on the ground, and at intervals Mrs Ilam held it up high so that it illuminated the faces of mother and son. They came into the middle of the avenue. It was now seriously raining.

"I knew it wouldn't be there," Ilam whispered, in an awed tone. "It isn't the sort of thing that stays. But I saw it – I saw the cloth and I saw a bit of its face."

Mrs Ilam looked about her.

"Nonsense, Jos," she upbraided him, fixing her eyes on him in a sort of reproof. "It's your imagination."

"It isn't," said Josephus. "I saw it; and what's more, it was on a bier. That's the worst – it was on a bier. Mother, he will haunt me all my life!"

"Don't talk so loud, child," put in Mrs Ilam. "You'd better go to bed."

"What's the good of going to bed?" he inquired. "What! I took him and I buried him as safe as houses. I left him there, and I came straight back here, except that I was stopped by a watchman at the stables, who told me the horses seemed to be all frightened. And I had a talk to the fellow; and I find it on a bier here, right in my path. And now it's gone again."

"Come in," said Mrs Ilam.

"And why were the horses frightened? That shows –"

"Come in," Mrs Ilam repeated. "I'll get you some hot milk, and you must try to sleep."

"Sleep!" he murmured. "Mother, you mustn't leave me."

And the procession re-entered the house, and the door was closed, but a light burned upstairs through the remainder of the night.

Carpentaria himself had little sleep; he scarcely tried to sleep. He arose at seven o'clock, and dressed and went out on to the balcony. The rain had ceased, and the Sunday morning was exquisitely calm and sunny. The whole scene was so bright and clear that the events of six hours ago appeared fantastic and impossible. Yet Carpentaria knew only too well that the unidentified corpse lay in the outhouse. He meant first to examine the corpse himself, and then to confide in a certain official of the City whom he knew that he could trust. What he should do after that he could not imagine. Decidedly some process of burial would be speedily imperative.

All the blinds of the Ilam bungalow were drawn. He guessed that at least the upper ones would remain so, and he was somewhat taken aback when Mrs Ilam herself appeared at a window and opened it. He was still more taken aback to see Mrs Ilam a moment later open the door, and with much stateliness cross the avenue to his own dwelling. He knew that she was friendly with Juliette, and that Juliette liked her. He, too, had admired her, but only because she was so old and so masterful, such a surprising relic. That she should be accessory to a crime did not seem strange to him. He esteemed her to be a woman capable of anything. He would have to warn Juliette.

At eight o'clock a servant brought up the French breakfast with which, under Juliette's influence, he compromised with hunger till lunch-time; and with the breakfast came, as usual, the cat Beppo. The breakfast consisted of a two-handled bowl of milk and a fresh roll and a pat of butter. Beppo seemed determined to share the breakfast without delay. Carpentaria, as was his frequent practice, took the roll off its plate and poured on the plate as much milk as it would hold. And Beppo, to whom milk was the answer to the riddle of the universe, leapt on to the table and began to lap in his gluttonous masculine way. He had taken exactly four laps when he ceased to lap. He looked up at his master, and there was a disturbed and pained expression in his amber eyes. This expression changed in an instant to one of positive fright. He was evidently breathing with difficulty, and he was rather at sea, for he groped about on the table and put both his forepaws into the bowl, splashing the milk in all directions. He then gave a fearful shriek; his pupils dilated horribly in spite of the strong sunshine, and he went into convulsions. His breath came quick and short. Finally, he fell off the table.

He was dead.

Less than three minutes previously he had been a cat full of power, of romance, and of the joy of life, with comfortable views on most things.

8

DISAPPEARANCE OF JULIETTE

People may read about crimes in newspapers all their lives, and yet never properly realise that crime exists. To appreciate what crime is, one must be brought to close quarters with crime, as Carpentaria was. Twelve hours ago murder to him had been nothing but a name. Now he knew the horror that murder inspires. And with the corpse of the cat Beppo lying at his feet, he felt that horror far more keenly even than in the night as he unearthed the corpse of the mysterious drunken man. He had actually seen the cat done to death, and, had it not been for the greediness of Beppo, he himself would have lain there, stretched out in eternal quiet.

He looked at the half-empty bowl of milk and at the splashes of milk on the round painted table, reflecting that each splash was no doubt sufficient to kill a man.

He wondered what he must do, how he must begin to disentangle himself from the coil of danger that was surrounding him. He was not afraid. He was probably. much too excited to be afraid. He was angry, startled, grieved, and puzzled, and nothing more. His mind turned naturally to Juliette – Juliette, his comforter and companion. He did not like the idea of frightening her by a recital of what had occurred, but he knew that he would be compelled to do so. He must talk confidentially to some one who understood him and admired him. Now, at that hour in the morning the faithful Juliette, her dress ornamented by an extremely small and attractive French apron, was in the habit of personally dusting the writing-table in Carpentaria's study adjoining the bedroom. No profane hand ever touched that table, and Juliette's own hand never ventured to arrange its sublime disorder. There were three servants in the house – the parlour-maid, the cook, and a scullery-maid. There might have been a dozen had Juliette so wished. But Juliette was a simple person; 'her father, the second husband of Carpentaria's mother, had belonged to the plain and excellent French bourgeoisie, who know so well how to cook and how to save money, and Juliette had inherited his tastes. Juliette was always curbing Carpentaria's instinct towards magnificence. She did not want even three servants, and there were a number of delicate tasks, such as the dusting of Carpentaria's table, that she would not permit them to do.

Carpentaria touched nothing on the balcony. He went into the bedroom, fastened the window, and then hesitated. He could hear Juliette's soft movements in the study. Ought he, could he, go to her and say bluntly: "Juliette, some one is trying to murder me, and you must take more care than you took this morning – you allowed my milk to be poisoned?"

At last he opened the door of the study.

But it was not Juliette dusting the sacred table. It was Jenkins, the parlour-maid!

Such a thing had never before happened in the united domesticity of Carpentaria and Juliette! It was astounding. It unnerved Carpentaria.

He locked the door of the bedroom, and put the key in his pocket,

"What are you doing here?" he demanded gruffly of the parlour-maid.

"Dusting your table, sir," replied Jenkins, in a tone that respectfully asked to be informed whether Carpentaria was blind.

"Who told you to dust my table?"

"Mistress, sir."

"Where is your mistress?"

"I don't know, sir. She told me to come up and dust the room." A pause. "I – er – really don't know."

"Go and find her. Ask her to speak to me at once."

"Yes, sir."

"Half a minute, Jenkins. It was you who brought my milk up?"

"Yes, sir."

"Where did you take it from?"

"Mistress gave it me with her own hands, sir."

"And you brought it direct to me?"

"Yes, sir."

"No one else touched it?"

"No, sir."

"Anybody called here this morning?"

"Called, sir?" Jenkins seemed ruffled.

"Yes. Anybody been to the house?"

"No, sir," said Jenkins, as though in asking if anybody had called Carpentaria was reflecting upon her moral character. And she blushed.

"Very well. Go and find your mistress."

Jenkins departed, and came back in a surprisingly short space of time.

Disappearance of Juliette

"Mistress doesn't seem to be about, sir," said Jenkins.

"What? She hasn't gone out, has she?"

"Not that I know of, sir. But I can't find her."

"Have you looked in her bedroom?"

"I knocked at the door, sir."

"And there was no answer?"

"No, sir."

"When did you last see your mistress?"

"When she told me to dust this room, sir, after I had brought up your milk."

"Where was she?"

"In the dining-room, sir."

A fearful thought ran through the mind of Carpentaria, cutting it like a lancet. Suppose that Juliette had been poisoned! Suppose that an attempt had been made against her, as against him, but with more success! He hurried out of the room and knocked loudly at her bedroom door.

"Juliette! Are you there?"

No answer.

"Julietta, I say!"

Again no answer. His heart almost stopped. He opened the door, and entered the room. It was empty, but already the bed had been made and everything tidied. He penetrated to the dressing-room, which was equally neat and equally empty.

Then he searched the house and the premises; he searched everywhere except in the little outhouse wherein was hidden the corpse of the drunken man. At length, after a futile cross-examination of the cook in the kitchin, he perceived that the' scullery-maid in the scullery was surreptitiously beckoning to him.

This ungainly chit, Polly, whose person was only kept presentable by the ceaseless efforts of Juliette, had red hair, rather less red than Carpentaria's, and she worshipped him afar off. She had that "cult" for him which very humble servants do sometimes entertain for masters who never even throw them a glance. And now she was beckoning to him and making eyes!

He followed her through the yard.

"Do you want mistress, sir?" whisper.

"Yes."

"Well, she's over the wye, sir."

"Over the way?"

"Yes, sir, at Mr Ilam's. Mrs Ilam's been here this morning, sir. Don't tell mistress as I told you, sir, for the love of heving!"

Juliette was at Ilam's! And he had twice found Juliette in the avenue during the night! And she had been strangely excited when she came to kiss him before going to bed.

In something less than fifteen seconds he was rattling loudly at Ilam's door. He received no answer. He heard no sound within the house. Wondering where the servants could be, he assaulted the door again, this time furiously. A man who was rolling a lawn in the Oriental Gardens glanced up at him. Still there was no reply. He was just deciding to break into the house by way of a window, when the door opened very suddenly, and as he was leaning upon it, he pitched forward into the hall and into the arms of old Mrs Ilam, who, with her white cap, her black dress and her parchment face, seemed aggrieved by this entrance.

"Mr Carpentaria!" she protested, raising her shaking hands.

But she was admirably and overpoweringly calm, and her extreme age prevented Carpentaria from taking the measures which he would have taken had she been younger, less imposing, less august, less like a dead woman who walked.

"My sister is here, and I must see her at once."

"No, Mr Carpentaria; your sister is not here."

Her tone startled him. It was so cold and positive. But after a few seconds he thought she was lying.

"She has been here, then?"

"No, Mr Carpentaria. She has not been here."

"Really! But you have seen her this morning. You came to my house."

"NO –"

"Excuse me, Mrs Ilam, I saw you from my –"

'' Ah! – from your balcony? You saw me cross the avenue, but you did not see me enter your house. You could not have seen that from your balcony, even if I had entered; and, as it happens, I didn't enter."

"My servants say you came."

"Your servants probably say a good many things, Mr Carpentaria," she smiled humorously.

The musician felt himself against a stone wall.

"Can I see your son?" he asked at length of the imperturbable old woman.

"My son is in bed and far from well," said Mrs Ilam.

"Then I should like to talk to you instead," said Carpentaria.

She seemed to burst into welcome.

"Come in then, my dear man, do! Come in!"

And she preceded him into the drawing-room, an apartment furnished in the richest Tottenham Court Road splendour. They sat down on either side of the hearth, where a fire was burning. He did not know exactly how to begin.

"Now, Mr Carpentaria," she encouraged him.

"Some very strange things have been happening, Mrs Ilam," said he.

He deemed that he might as well go directly to the point. He would come to Juliette afterwards. So long as Juliette was not in Ilam's house she was probably in no immediate danger.

"To you?" asked the dame.

"To me. I saw some very strange things with my own eyes last night, and within the last twelve hours there have been two attempts to murder me."

A slight flush reddened the wrinkled yellow cheek of Mrs Ilam. It seemed as though she tried to speak and could not. Her fingers worked convulsively.

"You, too?" she murmured, with apparent difficulty.

"Why do you say 'you, too'?" Carpentaria demanded.

She paused again.

"It was the milk?" she seemed to stammer.

"Yes, the second attempt; it was the milk," admitted Carpentaria.

She hid her face.

"The same attempt has been made against Josephus," she said. "And he was so frightened it made him ill. That is why he is not feeling very well this morning."

"But does Mr Ilam take milk for breakfast? I thought he always had Ilam and eggs?"

"Never!" said Mrs Ilam. "Hot bread-and-milk. Nothing else."

"And how did he find out that the milk was poisoned?" Carpentaria pursued.

"I – I don't know," said Mrs Ilam. "But he did. He's very particular about his food, is Jos. And he suspected something. So he tried it on Neptune, the Newfoundland. And Neptune is dead. He says he thinks it must be prussic acid. Oh, Mr Carpentaria, what is this plot against us all? What are we to do?"

Carpentaria was reduced to muteness. The old lady had changed the trend of his thoughts. He had been secretly accusing Ilam, but if Ilam's life also had been attempted, the case was very much altered. It was perhaps even more perilous. Still, Mrs Ilam had done nothing to explain the extraordinary events of the night. He decided to be cautious.

"I happened to see lights in your house very late last night, or rather, early this morning," he said. "I was afraid that either you or Mr Ilam might be ill."

His eyes sought hers and met them fully and squarely.

"Oh!" she exclaimed sadly. "Jos had a dreadful night. He does have them sometimes, you know. Bad dreams. In many ways he is just like a child. There are nights when I think his dreams are more real to him than his real life. Now, last night he dreamed there was a corpse lying on a bier in the avenue, and nothing would satisfy him but that I should come out with him to see. Fancy it! at my age! However, there was nothing – of course."

Carpentaria said to himself that the old lady evidently was unaware of her son's midnight escapade, and that he could get no further with her. The hope sprang up within him that Polly had been after all mistaken. Juliette might have gone out merely for a stroll and have returned ere then. He rose to take leave of Mrs Ilam.

"What are you going to do?" she asked him.

"What about?"

"Well, my dear man, about this attempted poisoning."

"I suppose we must inform the police," he replied.

"Yes, I suppose so," she agreed. "But perhaps it would be well to wait until you had had a talk with Jos. He'll be getting up during the day."

"We'll see," said Carpentaria.

"It's a good thing it's Sunday and we're free, isn't it?" she remarked.

He had got precisely as far as the drawing-room door, when a voice reached his ears from the upper storey. "Mrs Ilam! Mrs Ilam! He's eaten his Ilam and eggs. What about the marmalade?"

Carpentaria dashed into the hall and looked up the stairs, and he saw the head of Juliette over the banisters.

Behind him he heard a suppressed sigh from Mrs Ilam.

9

THE DEAD DOG

Carpentaria ran up the stairs. If he had not had flame-coloured hair, and the fiery temper that goes with it, he would probably have pursued the more dignified course of calling Juliette down and interrogating her in privacy. But he was Carpentaria. She knew his moods, and she fled before him into a sitting-room, where Ilam, a dressing-gown covering his suit of Sunday black, reclined in an easy-chair by the side of a small table bearing an empty plate and a knife and fork.

She cowered down on the floor.

"Oh, Carlos!" she exclaimed under her breath.

Carpentaria made the obvious demand:

"What are you doing in this house, Juliette?"

There was a silence.

"Look here, Carpentaria," Ilam began, rising a little in his chair.

"Silence!" cried Carpentaria angrily and threateningly.

And at the noise the great dog Neptune, pride of the Ilams, emerged from behind the chair and growled.

Juliette said at last:

"Mrs Ilam told me that Jos – that Mr Ilam was unwell, and so I – I came to see how he was. That's all."

"Really!" said Carpentaria. "Is that all? Your philanthropic interest in the sick and suffering, my girl, does you great credit.

But as the invalid seems to be doing fairly well you'd better come home with me, I want to talk to you."

Juliette gave a look of appeal to Ilam.

"I must tell him," she whispered. "I must tell Carlos. Why did you want me to keep it a secret? Carlos, Mr Ilam and I are engaged to be married. We love each other. We only want your consent, and Jos was afraid you mightn't give it. He was afraid. We've been engaged three days now, haven't we, Jos?"

"My consent!" Carpentaria shouted bitterly. "My consent!" His wrath was dreadful, and yet to a certain extent he was controlling himself. "I suppose," he addressed Juliette, "it's your love for this estimable gentleman that leads you out into the gardens of a night, and I suppose you take beautiful romantic moonlight strolls together. My consent! Ye gods!"

The dog continued to growl.

Juliette gathered herself together, and moved to Ilam's chair, and Ilam took her hand protectively.

"My poor dear! Never mind!" murmured Ilam soothingly.

Genuine affection spoke in those tones uttered by the stout and otherwise grotesque Mr Ilam. Love itself unmistakably appeared in the attitude of the pair as they clasped hands in front of Carpentaria's fury. And Carpentaria could not but be struck by what he saw. It sobered him, puzzled him, diverted his thoughts.

"Come, Juliette," he said in a quieter, more persuasive tone.

He turned to leave the room, and Juliette obediently followed. Allowing her to pass before him, he stopped an instant and threw a glance at Ilam.

"So they've been trying to poison you, Ilam."

"Poison me!" repeated Ilam, plainly at a loss.

"Yes," said Carpentaria with a sneer. "And you never have Ilam and eggs for breakfast. That's the reason why that plate is streaked with yellow. You always have milk. Naturally, you eat it with a knife and fork. And you suspected the milk and gave some of it to Neptune, and he fell down dead. He looks dead, doesn't he?"

"I don't know what you mean," Ilam said.

"You must ask mamma," replied Carpentaria, departing.

He saw now with the utmost clearness that the aged Mrs Ilam had been indulging him with some impromptu lying, invented, and clumsily invented, to put him off the scent, were it only for a few hours.

"She may be clumsy in her lying," he thought as he descended the stairs in Julliette's wake, "but she can act, the old woman can!"

He remembered that her acting had been perfect, and if Juliette had not happened to disclose the fact of her presence, the lying of Mrs Ilam, clumsy as it was, might have succeeded. It is so easy to poison a dog, and to arrange the remains of poisoned milk.

He was capable of congratulating her on her acting, but she had utterly vanished from the ground-floor.

When he had deposited Juliette safely in his study, she began to cry softly. It was impqssible for him to maintain his anger against her.

"Juliette," he said, "why do you have secrets from me?"

"Oh, Carlos, he wished it to be kept secret. He said he had reasons; and I love him. No one has ever loved me before, and I'm thirty."

"What about my affection?" asked Carpentaria.

"Oh, that's different!" she cried.

Then he questioned her about Mrs Ilam.

"I was at the kitchen window, preparing your milk, and the window was open, and Mrs Ilam came up outside, and told me that Jos was unwell, and wanted to see me."

"Did she touch the milk?"

"Touch the milk? No; why should she touch the milk?"

"Could she reach to touch the milk, supposing she had wished to?"

"I dare say she could. Yes, she could. But why?"

"Could you swear absolutely she didn't?"

"I couldn't swear; but I'm nearly sure. Carlos, what do you mean?"

"I'll show you what I mean!" said Carpentaria.

He unlocked the bedroom door and led her to the balcony.

10

A Pinch of Snuff

Three hours later Carpentaria, whose thoughts had been bent upon some solution of the problem set by Juliette's strange and incomprehensible love affair with Josephus Ilam, was obliged to devote his brains to other and not less disturbing matters. He received in his study, for the second time that day, young Rivers, the newly admitted doctor who had been officially attached to the City of Pleasure. A medical cabinet and a pharmacy had been judged quite indispensable to the smooth running of the City, and the foresight which had provided them was entirely justified by the numerous small accidents, faintings, and indispositions that marked the opening day, when more than three hundred persons had patronised the pharmacy, and more than twenty had received the attentions of the ardent young doctor.

Carpentaria had first met young Rivers when this youth was walking Bart's, and the accession of Rivers to the brilliant and brilliantly remunerated position of physician and surgeon-in-ordinary to the City of Pleasure was due to Carpentaria's influence. Rivers was grateful, very grateful. Moreover, he liked Carpentaria, thought him, in fact, the most wonderful man, except Lord Lister, that he had ever met.

"Well," said the fair youth of twenty-five, when Carpentaria had shut the study door, "I've made the analysis. It comes out to just about what I expected."

"Prussic acid?"

"Not exactly prussic acid. A soluble cyanide – cyanide of potassium. Have you by any chance got a photographic bureau concealed somewhere in the show?"

"Why, of course," said Carpentaria. "Didn't you know? It's next door to the lecture-hall."

"Then the cyanide of potassium was probably got from there. It's used by photographers. Better make inquiries."

"We will," Carpentaria agreed. "And do you mean to say cyanide of potassium will kill like that? How much prussic acid does it contain?"

"Scarcely any. Not two per cent. – not one per cent."

"And poor Beppo was dead in a minute."

"My dear Mr Carpentaria," said Rivers excitedly. "The strongest solution of prussic acid known to commerce only contains four per cent, of pure acid. And in the anhydrous state – "

"Anhydrous?"

"That means without water. In the anhydrous state," Rivers proceeded enthusiastically, "two grains will kill a man in a second of time. Like that! It's an amazing poison!"

Carpentaria shuddered.

"By the way," he said, as if casually, "I've got a corpse I want you to look at."

"A corpse?"

"Keep calm, my young friend," Carpentaria enjoined him. And he told him the history of the drunken man. "Naturally all this is strictly confidential," he concluded.

"I should think so," said Rivers, aghast. "Can you not see that you have got yourself into a dreadful mess? You are an accessory after the fact. You have been guilty of a gross illegality. I don't know what the penalty is; I'm not very well up in medical jurisprudence; but I know it's something pretty stiff. Why, you might be accused of the murder."

"Yes, l am aware of all that," answered Carpentaria. "But I was very curious; and I didn't want any police meddling here."

"You are going just the way to bring them here."

"Not at all. When you have made your examination I shall simply put the body where I found it. No one will be the wiser."

"And then?"

"Then – we shall see. It will depend on your examination."

"But, really, Mr Carpentaria, I cannot lend myself –"

"Not to oblige me?"

Carpentaria smiled an engaging smile, and they descended together to the outhouse.

The outhouse was not more than eleven feet square, and the barrow with its burden was stretched across it diagonally, so that when the two men were inside, the place was full and the door would scarcely close. A small window gave light.

Rivers gently pulled the black cloth aside.

"This is just such black cloth as photographers use," he remarked.

"So it is," said Carpentaria.

The eyes of the corpse were closed; he might have been a man asleep, this strange relic from which a soul had flown and which would soon resolve itself into its original dust.

"Poor fellow," thought Carpentaria. "Once he lived, and had interests, and probably passions, and thought himself of some importance in the universe."

The spectacle saddened Carpentaria, whereas the young doctor was not at all saddened, he was merely intensely interested.

"A blow on the head among other things," he observed, indicating to Carpentaria the top of the skull which showed an abrasion together with an extravasation of blood, now clotted.

"Would that do it?" queried Carpentaria.

"Don't know. Might. By Jove, the rigor is extraordinarily acute."

"Rigor."

"The stiffness that follows death. Great Scott!"

The doctor assumed an upright position, and stared, first at the corpse and then at Carpentaria.

"Great Scott!" he repeated.

"What's up?"

The doctor made no reply, but tried to lift the left arm of the body. He could not, without raising the entire body.

"This is most interesting," he said.

"What is?"

Again Rivers did not answer. Instead, he took his watch from his pocket, and put it suddenly against the ear of the corpse.

The corpse twitched; its head moved slightly; the eyelid lifted the eighth of an inch.

"See that? You're lucky! And so's he!" said the doctor. "It's catalepsy! that's all – A sudden slight noise at the ear itself will often produce a change of position in catalepsy."

"Then he's not dead!" exclaimed Carpentaria.

"Dead? He's no more dead than you are! It's just catalepsy, induced probably by that blow. But he must have been very excited previously, and, no doubt, suffering from melancholia too. My dear Mr Carpentaria, there is only one absolutely reliable symptom of death, and that is – putrefaction. Death is imitated by various diseases. But there are not many that will imitate the coldness of death as catalepsy will. Feel that hand; it's like ice."

"And how long will he remain in this condition?" asked Carpentaria, full of joy and relief.

"Till you go and bring me some snuff. Snuff is the best thing in these cases."

"And he'll be perfectly well again?"

"Yes, in a day or two."

"He'll remember – things?"

"Of course he will! Shall I go for that snuff, or will you?"

"I will run," said Carpentaria, and he ran.

11

THE RETURN TO LIFE

It was half-past seven o'clock on Monday evening. More than thirty hours had elapsed since young Rivers first began his operations to restore life to the cataleptic patient, and he was only just succeeding in an affair which had proved extremely difficult and protracted. Young Rivers, in fact, had found out during the watches of Sunday night and the sunny morning of Monday that the disease (if catalepsy may be called a disease) has a habit of flatly defying the rules of medical text-books and the experience of even the youngest doctors. But ultimately he had triumphed, though not by means of the famous snuff, which Carpentaria had obtained, after exhaustive research, from a bass-fiddle player in his band.

The patient reclined, alive, conscious, capable of movement and speech, but otherwise a prodigious enigma, in an arm-chair in Carpentaria's bedroom. His existence was a profound secret from all except the doctor and the musician.

And now these two, who had brought him back to earthly life, wanted him to talk, to explain himself, to unravel the mysteries of Saturday afternoon and Saturday night. And Carpentaria, dressed in his uniform, waited, watch in hand; for in half an horn-the daily concert must commence in the Oriental Gardens. Nothing could interfere with Carpentaria's presence in the gorgeous illuminated bandstand. He had sacrificed his interest in his half-sister, his curiosity about the doings of the Ilams, his inspection of the affairs of the City, and even a rehearsal, to the care of the recovering cataleptic, but the concert itself, with its audience of a hundred thousand or so, could not be sacrificed.

"So you are Carpentaria?" murmured the patient, sipping at a glass of hot milk.

His age now appeared to be fifty. He had grey hair and a short grey beard, rather whiter than the hair, and his eyes bore the expression of a man who has found that life bears no striking resemblance to a good joke. His hands moved nervously over the surfaces of the chair.

"Yes," Carpentaria admitted; "and you?"

It was the first direct question that he had ventured to put to the enigma, and the enigma ignored it.

"You say I was buried and you unburied me?" he pursued.

"Yes," said Carpentaria enthusiastically, and he described the journeys, the disappearances and the reappearances, of the body of the enigma on the opening night.

"I suppose I should have died really, if I'd been left alone?" the enigma demanded of Rivers.

"Undoubtedly," said Rivers. "Undoubtedly," he repeated.

The enigma turned almost fiercely on Carpentaria.

"Then why, in the name of common sense, couldn't you have left me alone?" tie cried.

It was as though he owed Carpentaria a grudge which the most cruel ingenuity could not satisfy.

"I – I thought –" Carpentaria stammered, too surprised to be able to argue well.

"You thought you were doing a mighty clever thing," snapped the enigma.

"I merely –"

"Or, rather," the enigma proceeded, "you didn't think at all."

Rivers and Carpentaria exchanged a glance, indicating to each other that the man was an invalid and must therefore be humoured.

"Really, Mr –" Carpentaria began.

"Call me Jetsam," the invalid interrupted. "It isn't my name, but it's near enough."

"Well, Mr Jetsam –"

"Not at all," said Mr Jetsam, sitting up in the chair. "There I was, comfortably dead, blind and deaf for evermore to the stupidities, the shams, the crimes, and the tedium of this world, and you go and deliberately recreate me! Is your opinion of the earth, and particularly of England, so high that you imagine a man is better on it than off it? Have you reached your present position and your present age, without coming to the conclusion that a person once comfortably dead would never want to be alive again? It seems to me, that you took upon yourself the responsibility, the terrible responsibility, of putting me back into life without giving the matter a moment's serious thought. And I do verily believe that you expected me to be grateful! Grateful!"

"It was a question of duty –" Carpentaria ventured.

"Yes, of course. It only remained for you to drag in that word; I anticipated it. And why was it your duty? Who told you it was your duty? What authority have you for saying it was your duty? None – absolutely none! The sole explanation of your conduct is that, like most human beings, you are an interfering busybody; you can't leave a thing alone."

At length Carpentaria laughed. He was conscious of a certain liking for Mr Jetsam.

"I can but offer you my humble apologies," he said. "They are of no avail; they will not undo what is done. But none the less I offer them to you. You see, when I last saw you alive, you were so drunk, so very drunk –"

"I was not drunk at all," said Mr Jetsam. "And your inability to perceive the fact proves that, though you may be able to wear a very stylish uniform and to make a great deal of noise with a band, you are an infant as a detective. No, sir, I had certain plans to execute, and you, with that meddlesomeness that appears to characterise you, came along and interfered. In order that I might be left alone I pretended to be drunk. I have never been drunk in my life, which is conceivably more than you can say for yourself, or you, sir" – and he pointed to the young doctor, who had only recently finished being a medical student.

"And those plans – may one inquire?" Carpentaria murmured.

Mr Jetsam covered his face with his hands.

"Ah!" he sighed, evidently speaking to himself. "I had done with all that, and now I must begin again. My instincts will inevitably drive me to begin again. My dear people" – he surveyed his two companions with an acid and distant stare – "instead of saving life, you have only set in motion a chain of circumstances that will lead to the loss of it. Murder and the scaffold will probably be the net result of your officious zeal."

There was a rap on the bedroom door.

"Five minutes to eight, sir," called a voice.

"Right," said Carpentaria, getting up; and to Mr Jetsam, "I will see you after the concert."

"I doubt it," said Mr Jetsam.

"Why not?"

"Because I shall be gone. I am feeling quite strong."

"I should like to talk to you about certain people," pursued Carpentaria.

"Who?"

"Well, Josephus Ilam."

"I know all about Josephus Ilam."

"And his mother. Perhaps you don't know all about his mother."

Mr Jetsam jumped to his feet with singular agility.

"Mrs Ilam! She's been dead for years," he said gravely.

"She was very much alive this morning," replied Carpentaria.

"He told me she was dead," Jetsam muttered.

"He lied. She is in the bungalow opposite."

"Oh!" Jetsam breathed, and he seemed to breathe the breath out of his body. He swayed and fell back into the chair.

"By Jove! He's fainted!" exclaimed Rivers.

"Look after him," said Carpentaria, and flew downstairs and towards his bandstand.

12

ON THE WHEEL

The concert was over. If it had been as great a triumph as usual
– and it had – the reasons were perhaps that nothing succeeds
like success, and that the Carpentaria band was so imbued with
the spirit of Carpentaria that it would have played in the
Carpentaria manner even had the shade of Beethoven come
down to conduct it. Certainly Carpentaria's performances with
the baton, though wild and bizarre, lacked that sincerity and
that amazing invention which usually distinguished them. He
had too much to think about. There was the possibility of
getting shot as he stood there. There was the possibility of being
poisoned at his next meal. There was the possibility of some
fearful complication with Juliette and Ilam. There was the
positive mystery of Ilam himself. There was the comparative
mystery of Ilam's mother. And there was the superlative
mystery of Mr Jetsam. Under these circumstances, with all these
pre-occupations, the plaudits of a hundred thousand people did
not particularly interest Carpentaria that night. His chief desire
was to get back to Mr Jetsam, and to extract Mr Jetsam's secrets
out of Mr Jetsam either by force, by fraud, or by persuasion. As
he was bowing languidly for the nineteenth time, and the entire
orchestra was bowing behind him, amid a hurricane of clapping,
he thought to himself:

"It's a good thing I'm not in love! It would only need that, in addition to what I really have on my hands, to drive me crazy!"

As a fact, he had never been in love. Art, particularly as expressed by brass instruments, was his mistress.

He turned to descend the steps from the bandstand, when he perceived a tall African standing at attention at the bottom of the steps.

"What do you want?" he asked the African.

The man smiled the placid and infantile smile of his race, and handed a note to Carpentaria.

"You from the Soudanese village?"

"Yes, sah."

The inhabitant of the Soudanese village, which was one of the attractions of the hippodrome, stood about six foot four inches high, and he was in native costume which consisted largely, but not exclusively, of beads and polish. To gaze, dazzled, at the polish on that man's face, shoulders, chest, and calves, one would guess that the whole tribe must sit up at nights bringing his polish to such a unique pitch of perfection. In his cheek you could see yourself as in a mirror, and he had the air of being personally well satisfied with the splendour of his mahogany skin.

Carpentaria opened the note. It read:

"Please come to me at once. – ILAM."

Should he go? Or should he refuse this strange invitation, and hasten at once to Mr Jetsam and the doctor?

On the Wheel

"Where is Mr Ilam?" he demanded of the Soudanese.

The Soudanese merely increased his smile, and pointed vaguely in the direction of the Amusements Park.

"Over there?"

"Yes, sah."

"But where, man?"

"Yes, sah!" He lifted an arm and pointed.

The upper part of the illuminated rim of the giant wheel, a hundred feet higher than any other wheel in the world, could be seen over the roofs of the lofty white buildings in the Central Way. At this moment a rushing, roaring noise was heard to the east, and simultaneously the lights of the giant wheel were extinguished. Carpentaria glanced round. A rocket burst with a faint reverberation in the sky, a little colony of crimson stars floated for a few seconds amid the clouds – some stars had the shape of the letter I and others of the letter C – and then they expired, and the sky was black again. Cheers greeted the ingenious signal for the commencement of the first pyrotechnic display of the City of Pleasure, and a small crowd, which was beginning to form in the neighbourhood of the Soudanese, frittered itself suddenly away in a rush towards the embankment.

The fireworks were discharged from a plot of ground on the other side of the river – a plot specially leased for that sole purpose.

"I'll come with,, you," said Carpentaria to the Soudanese. He had decided that an interview with Ilam could not do any harm, and there was always the chance that it might in some way prove decisive. As for Mr Jetsam, he would deal with Mr Jetsam later. Possibly Ilam might have determined to make a general confession to him.

And he had his revolver.

The Soudanese walked quickly, and he was several inches taller than Carpentaria. In something less than five minutes they had arrived at the entrance to the Amusements Park, which was closing for the night.

"Where is Mr Ilam?" Carpentaria asked again.

The Soudanese smiled.

They stood at the foot of the giant wheel, all of whose sixty cars were in darkness save one, and this car was at the bottom, and its door was open. Near the door stood a single official in the uniform of the City.

Carpentaria began to be puzzled.

"Mr Ilam at the top?" he asked the official.

"I think so, sir," said the official, after hesitating.

Carpentaria went into the car. The Soudanese shut the sliding door, remaining himself outside. The official blew a whistle, and the giant wheel began slowly to revolve with a terrific vibration and straining of chains and rods. The car was designed to hold sixty people – when the giant wheel was in full work it earned a hundred and eighty pounds per revolution – and Carpentaria felt lonely in it. "Is this some trap?" his thoughts ran; and he said to himself that he didn't care whether it was a trap or not. As the car rose in the sky he had a superb view of the fireworks, which were now in full career – an immense and glittering tapestry of changing coloured flame, reflected hue for hue and tint for tint on the calm surface of the Thames beneath. And high above the pyrotechnics lightning was beginning to play. The day had been hot, even close, and it had been a pleasing surprise to the money-takers of the City that rain had not fallen.

At last the wheel shuddered, shook, and stopped. The car was at the summit, three hundred and forty feet above the level of the earth. A figure appeared on the flying platform outside the car. The door was opened, and Ilam entered.

"What's the meaning of this?" Carpentaria demanded of him, standing up suddenly, and instinctively feeling the handle of his revolver with his right hand.

"It means that I wish to talk to you in private," answered Ilam, emphasising the last two words; "and there seems to me to be no place particularly private down below now," he added.

"What do you infer?"

"Perhaps I don't quite know what I infer," said Ilam. "All I can tell you is that this City has been getting rather peculiar this last day or two."

"It has," Carpentaria agreed pointedly.

"And as you went to the trouble of taking me up in that thing" – he indicated overhead, where the captive balloon was darting a searchlight to and fro across the expanse of the grounds – "I thought I'd go to the trouble of bringing you up here. It's safer."

Carpentaria noticed how pale the man was, how changed his visage, and how nervous his demeanour.

"I hope it is," said Carpentaria. "What do you want?"

"Let's sit down," replied Ram, clearing his throat, and they sat down on opposite sides of the car. "I'll explain what I want in three words. How much will you take to clear out? I'm a plain man – how much will you take to clear out?"

"Clear out of the City? I won't take anything," said Carpentaria. "All the gold of all the Rockefellers won't clear me out. I've got the largest audience for my band that any bandmaster ever had and I like it. It's worth more than money to me."

"Is it worth more than life to you?" asked the heavy President, gloomily.

"No; but I reckon I can keep my life and my audience, too," said Carpentaria. "At any rate you've tried to have my life twice and failed, and that hasn't frightened me. I'm less frightened than you are, even."

"I've not tried to kill you," said Ilam.

"You've tried to shoot me and to poison me. Why, I cannot imagine."

"I've not," repeated Ilam.

And, in spite of himself, Carpentaria was impressed by the apparent truthfulness of Ilam's tone.

"Then who has?"

"I've no idea," said Ilam lamely. "I don't know what you mean, what you are referring to. But I'll give you fifty thousand a year for ten years to go – to go."

"No," said Carpentaria. "I'm here. I stay."

"Then, you'll take the consequences."

"I always take the consequences. But what consequences, my friend?"

"Well," Ilam coughed, "you say there have been attempts on your life. Suppose they are continued? What then? I should like to save you. And perhaps I can only save you by persuading you to vanish."

"Awfully good of you," Carpentaria sneered.

"But I assure you that these attemps on my life interest me enormously. I wouldn't miss them for a fortune. I'm beginning rather to like them. One gets used to an atmosphere of mystery. No, Mr President, I shall not go; but Juliette will go. I shall send Juliette away to-morrow."

Ilam bit his lip.

"That remains to be seen," said he. "She likes me. I should make her a good husband. Why do you object to me?"

"Why do you court her in the dark? Why do you force her to have secrets from me?"

"That's neither here nor there," said Ilam. "I should make her a good husband."

"But what sort of a mother-in-law would she have if she married you?" demanded Carpentaria.

Ilam made no reply.

"And," continued Carpentaria, "I don't think it's a good thing for a woman to have a husband who is always seeing ghosts."

"Seeing ghosts."

"Don't you see ghosts?" sneered Carpentaria.

"N – no."

"Come down with me, and I will show you one, then," said the bandmaster.

He had conceived the idea of confronting Ilam with Mr Jetsam.

The shifting searchlight from the balloon fell dazzlingly across the car, and through the window Carpentaria saw plainly for the fraction of a second the polished face of the Soudanese. Then it disappeared.

He rushed to the door, flung it open, and gazed downwards into the weblike tracery of the steel-work which shone dully in the white glare of the searchlight. A zigzag stairway, incomparably slender, stretched away towards earth along the face of the colossal wheel, and a dark figure slipped rapidly from rung to rung of the dizzy ladder. Then the light moved capriciously away, and all was indistinguishable blackness.

13

PERFORMANCES OF MR JETSAM

Carpentaria slipped back into the car with a shiver, as it occurred to him that Ilam, had he so chosen, might have pushed him into three hundred and forty perpendicular feet of space. But Ilam had not moved.

"I've had enough," said Carpentaria. "We'll descend. Ring the bell."

"No," said Ilam. "I want to –"

"We'll descend," Carpentaria insisted.

"It's about Juliette," pleaded Ilam.

"We'll descend," said Carpentaria a third time. "Ring the bell."

He sat down, took his revolver from his pocket, and put it ostentatiously on his knees.

Ilam sighed, and pushed the white disc that communicated with the engine-house, and a few moments later a vibration went through the wheel, and it resumed its revolution. The car came down on the side nearest the river, and its occupants had a superb view of the final items of the display of fireworks. Among them were two portraits, in living flame, of the twin gods of the City of Pleasure, and under each headpiece was the name of its Subject: "Ilam," "Carpentaria." The cheers of the immense multitude greeted their ears. Then there was another

74

sound, but it came from above instead of from below. Ilam shrank as if afraid.

"You needn't be frightened," said Carpentaria. "It isn't the trumpet of the Day of Judgment, it's only the beginning of a thunder-storm. It's just come in nice time to soak everybody through on their way home."

Rain spattered viciously on the windows.

When they reached the ground a strange sight met their eyes – the sight of seas and oceans of black, shining umbrellas, surging in waves from all directions towards the Central Way and the exits from the City, and as the umbrellas reached the covered footpaths of the Central Way they collapsed and showed human beings,. And then, at all the exits from the City, all these umbrellas – and it was estimated that there were over a quarter of a million of them – sprang again into life, and hid their owners. The tempest was already at its height.

"Come with me," said Carpentaria, as Ilam sought to leave him, when they quitted the Amusements Park.

"No," said Ilam flatly.

They stood side by side in the open, heedless of the rain, while shelter in the shape of the side-walks of the Central Way was within a few yards of them. The searchlight from the balloon still swept about the grounds, but the fireworks were finished.

"You shall come with me and see a ghost," insisted Carpentaria angrily and obstinately, "or I will make such a scandal in this place as will go far to ruin it. Let me tell you that I know a great deal more than you think. I am in a position, for example, to ask you, Ilam, whether you spend your nights in bed or Performances of Mr Jetsam wandering about the grounds carrying mysterious burdens."

A group of visitors hurried past them.

"What do you mean?" muttered Ilam. "I – you must be going off your head."

"Doubtless I'm a madman, eh? Well, come along with the madman."

Ilam sighed. They passed into the Central Way, and had to fight for progress against the multitudes that crowded the footpaths. No one recognised them.

"I wish we could understand each other," said Ilam.

"We shall, rest assured of that," returned Carpentaria. "In quite a few minutes we shall understand each other, or I am mistaken, and it may be you that will have to leave this City – and with considerably less than fifty thousand a year, my friend."

He pictured the moment when he should confront Ilam with the man whose corpse Ilam had buried. Vistas opened out before him. He saw the tables completely turned; he saw himself sole master of the City, and the wielder of such power over Ilam as would enforce obedience to his wishes. Then there would be no more insulting requests to abandon his music, no more ridiculous suggestions, and no fear of foolishness on the part of Juliette. It astonished him that he had not realised before the enormous latent power which his knowledge of Saturday night gave him over Ilam.

"You will come with me to my house," he said.

"Who is there?" asked Ilam wearily.

"Dr. Rivers – and the ghost."

"What is all this nonsense about a ghost?"

"You shall see him first, and then, when you have seen him – before he has seen you – you shall tell me whether or not you would like to have a chat with him. It is a ghost warranted to talk."

Ilam said nothing. He was naturally at a complete loss.

They entered the bungalow by means of Carpentaria's latchkey, and they mounted to the first-floor and they went into the study. The door of the bedroom was shut. Carpentaria led Ilam out on to the balcony of the study window, from which it was not difficult, even for Ilam, to climb into the balcony of the bedroom.

"Now, you shall look into my bedroom," said Carpentaria.

And he himself looked first. It may be said that he was astounded.

The room was lighted. There was no signs of Mr Jetsam, but two chairs had been overturned, and young Rivers lay prone on the floor, his eyes shut, and some blood flowing from a wound in his forehead.

Carpentaria sprang into the room, and, strange to say, Ilam followed him. The fact was that Ilam did really for the moment believe Carpentaria to be mad, and the bedroom to be the scene of some maniacal crime.

Just then Rivers came to his senses.

"That you, Mr Carpentaria?" he murmured, rubbing his eyes.

"Yes. What's happened? Where's Jetsam, as he calls himself? You're not seriously hurt, are you?"

At the name of Jetsam, Ilam caught his breath and took hold of a bedpost.

"Jetsam?" he repeated.

"You evidently recognise the name of my ghost," said Carpentaria, "though he isn't here."

"He bashed me on the head with a chair," said the doctor, sitting up and putting a handkerchief to his head, "and I suppose I must have – It can't be more than a minute or two since –"

"But what was he doing? Where's he gone?" inquired Carpentaria impatiently.

"He recovered consciousness quite quickly," answered Rivers, "and I gave him something to drink; then he asked me about Mrs Ilam, and I told him she lived with Mr Ilam here, and he grew very excited, and said he must go to her at once. I said he couldn't; I said you wouldn't allow that, and he pretended to agree; but it was only a pretence. He began to talk about other things, and then, all of a sudden, he sprang at me, and that's as much as I remember."

Without a word Carpentaria ran out downstairs and into the avenue. The door of Ilam's house stood wide open. He entered. In the hall he perceived that the door of the drawing-room was also wide open, and he entered the drawing-room. There was no light in the room save that of a match, and the match was held by Mr Jetsam. Mr Jetsam stood staring at Mrs Ilam, and Mrs Ilam sat motionless in her chair, apparently trying to articulate and not succeeding. An appalling fear shone in her eyes. No sound could be heard except the rattling of the rain on the French window.

Mr Jetsam turned, and in the same second he dropped the match. The room was in darkness. Then followed a crash of glass and splintering of wood, and a heavy fall in the apartment itself. With some trouble, Carpentaria found the electric switch and turned on the light. Mrs Ilam's lips were still trembling in a vain effort to speak. Her son lay stretched and whimpering at her feet. Mr Jetsam had vanished. The window was in ruins.

Dr. Rivers appeared. He had bandaged his forehead.

"She is paralysed!" said the doctor, when he had examined Mrs Ilam. "She will never again have the use of her limbs or her organs of speech. She will be able to see and to hear, that's all."

PART TWO

THE TWINS

14

ENTRY OF THE TWINS

It is a singular fact that the secondary stage of the drama which
I am relating was tremendously, vitally, influenced by the
marriage of Mr Luke Shooter, junior partner in Shooter's, a firm
of wholesale ribbon merchants in Cannon Street. Luke Shooter
did not know it. Luke Shooter had nothing whatever to do with
the drama; it is very probable that he never even heard of it,
except such trifling fragments as got into the newspapers.
Nevertheless, by the mere fact of marrying, Luke Shooter
unconsciously changed the course of events in the City of
Pleasure. For he was a man of broad views, and he liked people
to think well of him, and so it occurred that, at his suggestion,
the multitudinous staff of Shooter's was given a complete
holiday on the day of his marriage, and that day happened to be
Tuesday, May 4.

So much for Mr Luke Shooter.

Many of the employes spent the latter half of the day in the
City of Pleasure, which was now the rage, the craze, and the
vogue of London, and among these were the twin sisters,
Pauline and Rosie Dartmouth. Pauline and Rosie were typists in
the house of Shooter's. Their age was twenty-six. They were tall,
and rather slim; only Rosie, the younger, was not quite so slim
as Pauline. Pauline was dark; Rosie was inclined to fairness. In
the partnership between them Pauline supplied the common

sense, while Rosie supplied the gaiety; each supplied a considerable amount of beauty and charm, and a sum of thirty-five shillings a week. It is obvious that on a total income of three pounds ten a week, or a hundred and eighty-two pounds a year, two girls living together in a small flat, with sense and gaiety and full opportunity for acquiring ribbons at wholesale prices, may have a very good time and cut quite a pretty figure in the world. And this Pauline and Rosie certainly did manage to do.

They were orphans, and had been for a very long time.

They came to the City by the Tube from their flat in Shepherd's Bush, and Pauline put a florin down for the two of them at the northern entrance gates, just as though they had been ordinary visitors; as, in fact, at that moment they were. A few persons noticed them, but quite casually, and only because they were dressed – and well dressed – almost exactly alike. There are so many beautiful young women in London that Londoners seldom turn their heads to look at one. It is left to Frenchmen to rave about the blond charm of the Anglo-Saxon "mees." What exuberant objectives the Frenchman would find to express his delight if he penetrated further north, into Staffordshire, Lancashire, and Yorkshire, where ugly faces and bad complexions are practically unknown, it is impossible to guess.

The City of Pleasure met with the entire approval of Pauline and Rosie. As soon as they found themselves in the Central Way they began to get enthusiastic. The sun was shining, the flags were flying, the cable-cars were gliding, and thousands and thousands of visitors made gay the City. They had never before seen anything like the Central Way, with its colonnades, and its shops, and its coloured throngs, and its soaring, gleaming, white architecture.

"It's just as good as being abroad, isn't it?" said Rosie.

"Better," said Pauline.

But then they had never been beyond Boulogne.

They stopped at shop windows, as much to regard jewellery and knick-knacks, as to observe whether their frocks and chiffons and hats were in that immaculate order which a sunny day and the presence of one's fellow-creatures demand. It may be mentioned here that their dresses were of dark blue, with blue belts, bunchy knots of white muslin at the throat, white gloves, brown glace kid boots, and large blue-and-black picture hats. It was plain, but it was perfect, and they knew it was perfect. The consciousness of perfection enabled them to sustain the judicial gaze of other women, and the passing glance of innumerable young men, with a supercilious stare. In truth they were secretly wild with the joy of life, and the attractiveness of the City, and the sensations of their holiday, but they did not show it. Oh, no! They did not show it. They were prim to the most advanced degree, as became them.

"I should just love to go on one of those dear little cable-cars!" exclaimed Rosie.

"Well, let's," Pauline agreed.

"Aren't they delicious?" said Rosie.

And only in the girlish hop, skip, and jump, which landed them gracefully on a car, was there a hint of the pent-up vivacity which surged in their veins – a hint that vanished as rapidly as it had showed itself. As Rosie smoothed out her skirt, and as Pauline opened the purse in her gloved hand to give two pence to the conductor, they had the utter demureness of duchesses.

The car was open to the sky, with crosswise seats, and, as it sailed rapidly down the Central Way, constantly passing other cars coming in the opposite direction, and passing fountains and flower-beds and elephants and camels, and all the strange world of the City, the pleasure became rather too keen for Rose's mercurial heart. She took Pauline's hand and pressed it, sitting a little bit closer to her.

"Suppose we meet him?" she whispered.

"What? In this crowd? Never! Besides, he isn't likely to be outside," said Pauline.

She was only a few minutes older than Rosie, but she could not have played the elder sister more completely had she been ten years older.

"We might meet *her*, anyway!" murmured Rosie.

"Nonsense, Rosie. You don't imagine she'll be here, do you?"

"I don't know," said Rosie, lifting her chin. "But suppose we do meet him, or either of them."

"Well, then," said Pauline wisely, " we meet them, that's all."

"Shall you speak to them?" Rosie asked; "I shan't."

"We'll think about that when we see them," said Pauline.

"Oh!" cried Rosie.

This exclamation had nothing to do with the foregoing chatter. It merely expressed some part of Rosie's joy when the car came to the magnificent circular place half-way down the Central Way, with the fa9ade of the Exposition Palace on the right, the stately entrance to the Oriental Gardens on the left, and the superb vista of the thoroughfare before and behind.

"Oh!" cried Rosie again, for quite a different reason.

Already she had forgotten the architecture, and other beauties of this scene, and was eagerly directing Pauline's attention to a tall man with vivid hair and an individual style, who had just crossed the rails in front of the car and was proceeding towards the Oriental Gardens.

"There!" said Rosie, pointing frantically, yet primly. "Don't you see him?"

"Who? That man with the red hair?"

"Yes; it's Carpentaria, isn't it?"

"So it is, I do declare!" agreed Pauline, frankly as interested as her sister.

It was.

"Oh!" breathed Rosie regretfully, as the car swept them further from the figure of the popular hero. "Doesn't he look lovely? He's just like his portraits, only nicer, isn't he?"

"I – I couldn't see him very well," said the discreet Pauline.

"Yes, you could," Rosie corrected her sharply. "You know you adore him. But you're always so mum."

Pauline smiled placidly.

"I do wish we could meet him – be introduced to him I mean!" said Rosie.

"My dear child," Pauline reprimanded. "Don't be silly. He's frightfully rich." " I know!" said Rosie sadly. "But he isn't married. I think his hair's beautiful."

In common with very many English and other girls, Rosie and Pauline were capable of displaying brazenly, for a man they had scarcely seen, an affection the tenth part of which certain males with whom they were intimately acquainted would have been delighted to receive. Their virgin hearts had never been touched, not even by the Apollos of the house of Shooter; they prided themselves on their unapproachableness; yet they could rave about Carpentaria, and openly profess that they were his slaves. In Carpentaria's presence they would doubtless have behaved, even if they did not feel, differently.

The car whirled them to the other end of the City, and they began systematically to do everything and to see everything that could be done and seen, from the captive balloon (not that they did that – they were content to see it) to the Soudanese native village, from the circus to the exhibition relating to Woman, from the cricket field to the Freak Show, and from the Art Galleries to the ladies' afternoon-tea cafe. They were in the ladies' afternoon-tea cafe, and paying for two pots of tea, seven cakes, and an extra cream, just as the clock struck five. It then occurred to them that a concert of military music began at precisely five o'clock in the Oriental Gardens, and they decided to go and listen to it, even though, sad to say, Carpentaria never conducted in person till the evening.

They crossed the Central Way, and were strolling along the avenue to the Gardens, when Pauline stopped. "Well, I never!" she exclaimed.

"What is it?"

Coming down the steps of Ilam's bungalow was the great Ilam himself, and it was to Ilam she pointed.

"What shall we do?" whispered Rosie. "He's lots older, isn't he?… And you said we shouldn't meet him!"

They walked on, irresolute and blushing, and just as they arrived opposite Ilam's gate, with their eyes gazing studiously straight in front of them, Ilam called out:

"Hi, there! Young ladies!"

Now, the avenue was generously sprinkled with people, but Pauline and Rosie happened to be the only young ladies within hail, and to have ignored such a loud and unmistakable appeal as Ilam's would have drawn down upon them more public attention than they desired. They therefore stopped, still blushing, but delightfully blushing, and smiling with that innate kindliness of heart which distinguished both of them. Rosie spoke first. She was a woman, and had positively stated that under the circumstances she should not speak. Hence, naturally, she spoke first.

"Good afternoon, cousin," said she.

In her manner of pronouncing that word "cousin," a non-committal manner, a more-than-meets-the-eye manner, a defensive manner – in a word a family manner – she indicated a whole family history. When relatives who are distant in more senses than one meet after a considerable period, that particular manner is invariably employed by the one who speaks first.

The history of the Dartmouths and the Ilams was quite simple – indeed, so usual as Jo be hardly worthy of record. Mrs Dartmouth, mother of the twins, had been an Ilam. She was an orphan child of Josephus' dead uncle, and therefore niece of Josephus' father. And before her marriage she was understood to have "expectations" from that mighty and opulent soda-water manufacturer. However, heedless of these expectations, she went and married beneath her – to wit a solicitor's clerk. The niece of a rich soda-water manufacturer has no business to marry a solicitor's clerk. The result was a complete estrangement.

Mrs Dartmouth gave all the Ilams to understand that she and her husband had no need of any one's money – that, in fact, they scorned the Ilam millions. Mrs Dartmouth met Josephus at his father's funeral. Ten years later Pauline and Rosie met Josephus at Mrs Dartmouth's funeral. They shook hands formally, and made it clear to Josephus that they would stoop to accept no gift from him, who had scorned their mother, even should he offer it.

That was seven years ago, and Pauline and Rosie were now absolutely alone in the world, and, moreover, age had taught them tolerance, and their curiosity had been extremely excited by the news of their cousin's partnership with the world-renowned Carpentaria, and the subsequent birth of the City of Pleasure. So that, in spite of anything they might have previously said to each other, they were rather pleased to meet their solemn cousin, who, after all, was a millionaire, and who really seemed less aloof and stiff than he appeared at funerals.

"So you were going to cut me?" said Ilam, trying to smile.

"No, cousin," said Pauline. "How are you? You don't look very well."

They shook hands over the gate.

"I'm not," said Ilam.

' "And Mrs Ilam. She keeps pretty well, I hope," put in Rosie decorously.

"That's just it. She doesn't. She's – Won't you come in?"

And he opened the gate.

"Do you live here?" cried Rosie. "Fancy living in the middle of this place! How jolly! And what a jolly house! Oh! what a delicious notion – living in the show!"

And they disappeared into the bungalow.

The historic family coolness looked as if it was going to warm itself into a sort of pleasant acquaintanceship.

15

PROPOSAL OF JOSEPHUS

"Yes," Ilam was saying when they came downstairs, "she has been like that since last night, and the doctors – I have had two – assure me that at her age no recovery is possible. She can take liquid food, and she can move her eyes slightly – you noticed how her eyes turn? – but otherwise she is incapable of movement, and, of course, she can't articulate."

He had taken his young relatives upstairs to see his mother, and the picture of her, lying almost in the attitude of a corpse on the bed, with a uniformed nurse sitting motionless beside her, had made a deep impression on Pauline and Rosie. In fact, the whole house saddened them. It was spacious and luxurious, but it was far from reaching that standard of splendour which one might reasonably expect from the Ilam wealth. Ilam did not look like a wealthy man. He did not talk like a wealthy man, and both girls began to perceive, dimly, that wealth is useless to those who have not sufficient imagination to employ it. Certainly the City of Pleasure was an expression of the Ilam riches, but they knew, as all the world knew, that the imagination which had brought into being the City of Pleasure was Carpentaria's. Hence, they felt sorry for Josephus Ilam, partly because of the calamity to his mother, and partly because of his forlorn and anxious air; they thought he wanted looking after, and that this heavy pompous man was greatly to be pitied, despite his opulence.

"You haven't told us how it happened, what caused it?" said Pauline sympathetically.

"Oh!" said Ilam, "as to that, who can tell? Probably some fright, some shock. But we can't say. She was alone when it happened. And as she can't speak – can't write – can't – Well, you see how it is."

"We are sorry for you," murmured Rosie. "And here I am, alone as it were," Ilam continued. "What am I to do? What can a man do by himself? I've got a nurse. I can get fifty nurses, if necessary. And there are the servants. But what are nurses and servants? You understand my position, don't you?"

"Yes, quite," said Pauline.

They were partaking of a second tea in the Ilam drawing-room. The appetite of Rosie for cakes seemed unimpaired, though she did her best to hide it, and to pretend that she was only eating cakes out of politeness.

Ilam swallowed his tea in great gulps. "I'm utterly unnerved," he said. "You must be," said Rosie kindly. "There's a vast amount of superintendence to do in the City, as you may guess. But what am I fit for, with my poor old mother lying up there? You can't fancy what she was to me. I depended on her for everything – everything."

And then tears showed themselves in the little eyes of Josephus Ilam. The appearance of those tears of a great strong man made Rosie feel very uncomfortable, so much so, that she was obliged to look out of the window.

"I wish we could help you," said Pauline, after a pause.

"We'd do anything we could," said Rosie.

Ilam glanced up.

"You can do everything," he said. "I hesitated to ask you, but since you've mentioned it yourselves…and I'll make it worth your while. Rely on that."

"But what?" demanded Pauline, startled, while Rosie put down a fresh piece of cake which she had just taken.

"Come and live here," said Ilam bluntly.

"Both of us?"

"Both of you."

"We couldn't do that, really," said Pauline.

"No, of course not. But wouldn't it be lovely?" added Rosie.

"Why couldn't you?" asked Ilam. "You are your own mistresses, aren't you? What is there to prevent you?"

"Well, you see," said Pauline judicially, "we have our living to get, and then there's our flat, and –"

"I don't know how much you earn," Ilam cried. "But I'll cheerfully undertake to give you treble, whatever it is."

"That would be five hundred and forty-six pounds a year, then," said Rosie, who was specially good at arithmetic.

"Let us say six hundred," Ilam amended the figure with a tremendously casual air.

The girls felt that, after all, perhaps he resembled a millionaire more than they had at first thought.

"Come, now," Ilam urged. "Say yes. It's an idea that came to me all of a sudden, while I was talking to you. But it's an idea that gets better and better the more I think about it."

"But we couldn't give up our situations," objected Pauline.

"Why not?" Ilam asked.

"I don't know," Pauline stammered. "It seems so queer. It's so sudden. What would our duties be here?"

"Your duties would be to act as mistresses of this house, and to look after my poor mother. Of course, there'd be a nurse as well. I don't know how many servants there are – five or six."

"And we should have to manage everything?" said Pauline.

"Everything domestic. Come, you agree?"

"But suppose," interpolated Rosie – "suppose we – you – we didn't suit you?"

What she meant was "Suppose you didn't suit us?"

"Come a month on trial," said Ilam. "At the end of that time, if you want to leave, I'll guarantee you a situation quite as good as you're leaving. I can't say fairer than that, can I?"

There was a pause; the twins looked at each other.

"Just think how I'm fixed!" pleaded Ilam.

"What do you say, Rosie?" Pauline asked primly of her sister.

"Well," answered Rosie, "as cousin is in such a dilemma, and poor Mrs Ilam so – so ill, perhaps –"

"Good!" exclaimed Ilam; "you agree. Good! I'm very much obliged to you. You're two really nice girls, and I can assure you you'll have a free hand here."

"You decide for us," said Pauline, smiling and reddening under Ilam's appreciation.

"We'll begin at once, eh?" said Ilam. "Tonight."

"Oh, that's quite out of the question," objected Rosie. "We shall be obliged to give a month's notice at Shooter's."

"Nonsense!" said Ilam. "I'll send 'em a cheque for a month's salary instead; then they can't grumble."

"But to-morrow? How will they manage without us?" persisted Rosie.

Ilam laughed – and it was not often that Ilam laughed. Either the humour of the thing must have appealed to him very strongly, or it was a symptom that his spirits had mightily improved.

"They'll manage without you," he said.

"It's true they can get substitutes from the Typewriting Exchange," said Pauline.

Thus, it was arranged that Pauline and Rosie should take one of the City automobiles to their flat, and return with trunks and boxes during the evening. Before leaving the bungalow Pauline wrote to Shooter's informing them of the blow that had fallen on Shooter's, and Ilam filled in a cheque, and Rosie put it in the envelope and fastened the envelope. The automobile ordered by telephone came round to the door.

"You'll introduce us to Mr Carpentaria, won't you?" said Rosie smilingly, as she was getting into the carriage.

Ilam frowned, and then cleared his face.

"Do you want to know him?" he asked.

"Why, of course!"

"Very well, I suppose you must," Ilam agreed.

"Well, isn't this the greatest fun?" Rosie whispered to Pauline when they drove off. "We can go where we like in the City. We can save at least five hundred a year, and perhaps we shall be his heiresses."

"Hush!" Pauline admonished her.

And three hours later those two extremely practical twins were thoroughly installed in the Ilam bungalow. They had the air of having lived there all their lives as they chatted with Ilam in the drawing-room. Ilam himself was decidedly looking a little better.

"I have been talking to nurse," said Pauline importantly, "and I shall sleep on the couch in Mrs Ilam's room to-night. Nurse needs rest. She says there is nothing to do, but some one should be there."

"I don't want you to begin by tiring yourselves," said Ilam, "but, of course –"

They heard a violent ring at the front door, and presently a servant entered. Ilam started.

"Mr Carpentaria," said the servant.

Ilam turned pale.

"Show him in," said Rosie calmly to the servant.

"Yes, Miss Rose," said the servant, who, in common with the other servants, had already been clearly informed of the names, position, and authority of the new-comers.

"You are to introduce him to us, you know," Rosie murmured sweetly to Ilam, "and I suppose we shall have to play hostesses now."

Carpentaria came in, evidently hot from his concert.

"I say, Ilam –" he began.

Then he perceived the twins," and Ilam clumsily performed the introductions. The girls were enchanted with his uniform and with him. He said little, and he was pale, but then he was so distinguished; all his movements were distinguished and magnificent.

"We saw you this afternoon," Rosie ventured, timidly.

"And I didn't see you! The loss was mine," he returned, gazing at Pauline.

Ilam had sunk back heavily into a chair. Carpentaria caught sight of his face, and an awkward silence followed.

"I came on a matter of business," Carpentaria said to Ilam, "but I won't trouble you now; it will do to-morrow. Goodnight."

"We shall hope to see more of you," said Rosie, when Carpentaria had demonstrated that he really meant to go.

"Yes, indeed," said Pauline very quietly, and the visitor bowed.

And then Carpentaria, that glorious vision, had vanished.

"Cousin's nerves are simply all to pieces," commented Rosie, as the girls were going upstairs; "even a casual visitor upsets him. Did you notice his face as soon as the bell rang?"

"Yes, poor thing!"

"But Carpentaria is a dear!" Rosie added.

Some time afterwards Pauline, in a dressing-gown, came into Mrs Ilam's bedroom, and the nurse left it. The cIlamber was large, with heavy mahogany furniture and a large window; a fire burnt in the grate. Pauline stood over the bed and smiled at her aged and stricken relative. The old woman lay on her back, in a white nightgown and white nightcap, and her arms were stretched straight downwards outside the quilt, parallel with her body. She was dead, except for her eyes, which burned brightly, and winked now and then.

"Are you all right?" Pauline asked comfortingly.

The eyes flashed.

"Cousin Ilam says you like to be read to. Shall I read to you before you go to sleep?"

The eyes flashed.

"Very well, then, I will."

Pauline took a book from a pile of books which lay on a chest of drawers. It was Frank R. Stockton's "The Lady or the Tiger?" and, sitting down on the edge of the bed, her face turned towards the fire, she began to read as follows:

"In the very olden time there lived a semi-barbaric King, whose ideas, though somewhat polished and sharpened by the progressiveness of distant Latin neighbours, were still large, florid, and untrammelled, as became the half of him which was barbaric."

She stopped. The eyes were blinking rapidly; then they blinked not quite so fast; then not at all.

"You want me to read more slowly? Very well."

She recommenced with great deliberation:

"In the very – olden – time –"

The eyes were blinking again furiously.

"What is it?" asked Pauline. "What can it be?"

Tears stood in those black gleaming eyes, and yet the face seemed annoyed rather than sorrowful; and as the eyes stared fixedly at the ceiling the horror of the mystery that surrounded Mrs Ilam swept over Pauline like a wave.

"Have I got to spend the whole night with those eyes?" she asked herself. "What is it they want to tell me?"

16

THE BOX

Pauline had put the book down on the bed, and was bending over the fire pulling the coals together with the poker. She performed this homely, natural, everyday action more to reassure herself, to convince herself that she was in an everyday world, than because the fire needed attention. For the strange mystery of the speechless creature on the bed, helpless as though bound with chains and gagged by the devices of torturers, had seized and terrified her. She held the poker in the air and listened. Not a sound save the ticking of the clock on the mantelpiece! From all the sleeping house, not a sound. She might have been alone with the living corpse in the house, and yet she knew that Rosie, and Josephus Ilam, and the nurse, and the half-dozen servants, were in various rooms of it, perhaps sleeping, perhaps trying to sleep.

There was a sudden sharp noise behind her, near the bed.

She started violently and glanced round in fear. It was merely the book – the harmless and amusing "The Lady or the Tiger?" – which had slipped from the bed to the floor. Yet how could it have slipped? Had the paralytic, who was incapable of the slightest movement, after all twitched a limb and so shaken the book off the bed? Absurd. She had merely placed the book too close to the edge of the bed; that was all. Nothing more natural, nothing more probable. Her nervous fright was grotesque.

She rose, picked up the book, and looked again at her charge. The burning, blazing eyes were still dropping tears, and the tears ran in a deep furrow down either cheek. Softly Pauline wiped them away, her own eyes moist. The tragedy of the life's end of this old, old woman, whom every one had regarded as fierce and formidable, rendered helpless in a moment by no one knew what horrible visitation, chilled her heart's core.

"What can she want? What is troubling her?" thought Pauline frenziedly.

And then she imagined that perhaps she had mistaken all the symptoms of those eyes, and that Mrs Ilam had wished her to continue to read. She resumed the book, and read very slowly in a fairly loud voice. And instantly the eyes began to blink irregularly – fast, then slow – and the eyeballs themselves moved slightly from side to side. Obviously the patient was not content.

Pauline put down the book again in despair.

The eyeballs still moved slightly to and fro.

"She wants something in the room. What can it be?" said Pauline to herself. "It may be she is thirsty."

She went to the night-table, and poured a few drops of water into the invalid's cup, and brought it near Mrs Ilam's lips. But the eyes seemed to close as if in refusal, and the face, which could only wear one expression – that of grief – to deepen its inexpressible melancholy.

And then an idea occurred to Pauline, and shone on her brow like a light.

"Listen," she said kindly to the aged woman. "I will ask you some questions. The answers will be only yes or no. If you mean ' no ' try to keep your eyelids still, but if you mean ' yes ' blink them as much as you can. Do you understand?"

The eyelids blinked; and then they continued their terrible entranced stare at a spot on the ceiling exactly above their owner's head.

"Good," said Pauline. "Are you in pain?"

No movement of the eyelids.

"Are you thirsty?"

A slight nickering, which the patient clearly endeavoured to suppress.

"You want something?"

The eyes blinked.

"Is it some person?"

The eyelids were steady.

"Something in this room?"

A violent blinking.

"Is it in a drawer?"

The eyelids were steady.

"Then I can see it as I stand here?"

The eyes blinked again. Pauline set the cup down on the night-table, and gazed round the room. She went to the mantelpiece, and gave a list of the things on it; candlestick, clock, matches, vases, keys, medicine-bottle, a piece of crotchet work, a long knitting-needle, a picture post-card. There was no response from the invalid.

"How foolish I am!" murmured Pauline. "She cannot possibly want any of these things." Then she saw a few old letters half-hidden behind the clock.

"Is it there?" she asked, holding the letters near to Mrs Ilam.

But there was still no response. She put back the letters and went to the ottoman, on which was a large family Bible. But it was not the Bible that Mrs Ilam wanted, nor a spectacle case that lay on the Bible. Then Pauline catalogued one by one the contents of the dressing – table, and the contents of the washstand, still with no result. At last, she came to a chest of drawers, covered with a piece of white crewel-work, and bearing some wax flowers, two small vases, a black lacquered box, sundry folded linen, several books, and a few faded photographs. She described the photographs and the linen and the books, as these seemed to be the most likely objects, and then she came to the lacquered box. And suddenly, the eyes began to blink furiously.

"You want this box?"

The eyes continued to blink.

She brought it to the bed. It was about eight inches square and three inches in depth, and beautifully inlaid with mother-of-pearl in a design to resemble a bunch of roses – just such a little cabinet as our grandmothers valued, such as was scorned as being Early Victorian during the aesthetic movement of the eighties and nineties, but such as we ourselves are beginning to recognise as beautiful. It had prominent brass hinges, and a keyhole, and it was locked.

"Do you want me to open it? It's locked."

The eyes were moderately still?-

"Then you wish it put somewhere else?"

They blinked.

"In a drawer?"

No response.

"On the dressing-table?"

No response.

"Near you?"

The eyes blinked.

"On the bed?"

No response.

"Under the bed?"

No response.

Pauline was at a loss.

"Under your pillow?" she hazarded at length.

The eyelids moved up and down, if not with joy, at any rate with satisfaction.

And very carefully Pauline raised the pillow, and Mrs Ilam's head, and slipped the box underneath both the pillow and the bolster.

"There; is that right?"

The tragic eyes blinked, and a slight sigh emanated weakly from between those thin pale lips. But, slight as it was, it seemed to have come from the innermost depths of the stricken woman's being. It might have been a sigh to indicate that her last wish was realised.

"I shall lie down now," said Pauline, and turning out all the electric lights except the tiny table lamp on the table, she stretched herself on the couch which stood at the foot of the great bed, and she drew a rug over her, and shut her eyes and told herself that she must sleep. But she could not sleep. Her brain was as busy as the inside of a clock, and electric lights seemed to be burning and fizzing it, extinguishing themselves and relighting themselves. What strange house had she and Rosie wandered into? What was the hidden secret of this paralysis, and of Josephus Ilam's worn and worried mien, and of the sudden arrival and equally sudden departure of Carpentaria? And, above all, what was the meaning of the old woman's desire for the box? What was in the box?

Do not imagine that Pauline regretted having come. She did not. Except under the passing influences of night and of the presence of illness, she was not a bit superstitious; nor was Rosie. They were not afraid of mysteries. They were intensely practical young women, incapable of being frightened or repulsed by what they did not understand. And that Pauline was a girl entirely without the timidity of the doe, she abundantly proved in the next few minutes. As she lay on the couch she could see, without moving her head, the French window. She fancied that the heavy crimson curtain was somewhat pulled aside in one place, at a height of about four feet from the ground, and she fancied that she could see the end of a finger on the end of the curtain. "No," she said to herself, "this is ridiculous. There cannot possibly be a finger there. I must not be silly," and she resolutely shut her eyes. The next time she opened them, the fire had blazed up a little and, more than

99

ever, the something on the edge of the curtain resembled a finger.

Her little heart beating, but courageously, she noiselessly rose up from the couch and approached the window.

It was the end of a finger on the edge of the curtain – a finger with a rounded and very white finger-nail! Moreover, the curtain trembled slightly, as it would do if held by some one who was endeavouring not to move. Pauline remembered that the French window "behind the curtain had purposely been left slightly open, and that it gave on to a balcony, as most of the windows of the bungalow did.

She advanced resolutely, and drew aside the curtain.

17

The Man on the Balcony

A man was standing behind it. The French window had been opened at least eight inches, and the man stood partly in the aperture and partly in the room. He did not flinch. He did not even seem scared, nor yet disturbed. He was a middle-aged man, with grey hair, and a worn, rather sad face, and he wore a blue suit of clothes, which showed earth-stains and other evidences of an exciting and violent life. He was, in fact, the man whom Ilam had buried, and who described himself to Carpentaria as Mr Jetsam.

"What are you doing here?" demanded Pauline, in a low, brave voice. "What do you want?"

She mastered her fear, though her heart was beating madly. She determined that, just as she had proved equal to difficult situations in the past, she would prove equal to this one.

"Now that you have seen me, I want to talk to you," replied the man.

"You climbed up by the balcony, didn't you?" she asked.

"Yes," said the intruder. "Nothing more simple. I found a ladder."

"Then you had better go as you came – and quickly!" said the girl.

"And the alternative?"

"Of course I must call the master of the house. In any event I shall do that."

"No," said Mr Jetsam. "For heaven's sake don't call Jos."

"Jos!" repeated Pauline, astounded at this familiarity.

"I said ' Jos,' " the man insisted firmly. "What do you take me for?"

"Naturally I take you for a burglar. What else should you be?"

"Now, do I look like a burglar?" Mr Jetsam asked severely. "Examine me, and tell me whether I look like a burglar."

"Whatever you are," said Pauline, in a tone of decision, "I cannot remain talking to you like this. I am in charge of an invalid here, and you must go."

The man gazed at her fixedly. She thought his eyes were very sad eyes, and yet dignified, too. They reminded her of the eyes of Mrs Ilam. And presently, when they grew moist, they reminded her even more of the eyes of Mrs Ilam.

"Miss Dartmouth," said the man, "I can easily prove to you that I am not a burglar."

"Then you know me?"

"I know of you. I know your name. I know you by sight. I know that you and your sister have come into this stricken and fatal house from sheer goodness of heart."

"Do not talk like that," said Pauline, whom any praise, save of her personal appearance, made extremely uncomfortable. She endeavoured to make her voice cold, forbidding, and accusatory, but she could not. The eyes of the grey-haired man seemed to hypnotise her, to rob her of initiative, and of the power to decide things for herself.

"I will talk in any manner you like," returned Mr Jetsam, "provided you will let me come into the room and explain to you what I want."

"Impossible," she replied.

"Why impossible? It is, on the contrary, perfectly easy," said Mr Jetsam. "All I have to do is to close the window" – and he closed it – "to come into the room" – and he came in –" and to ask you to be good enough to listen."

He put down his felt hat on a chair.

He now stood within the room, a couple of feet from Pauline, in the direction of the bed, but with his back to it.

Pauline, with a sudden sharp movement, darted to the mantelpiece, by the side of which was the bell-push. In the same instant he, too, darted forward and clutched her wrist, just as she was about to touch the bell. They held themselves rigid for a moment, like statues.

"I understand your feelings," said Mr Jetsam in a shaken voice. "I admire you. But before you ring that bell, let me assure you most solemnly that if you do ring it you will bring murder into this house. You will utterly ruin one family, if not two. Believe what I say; you cannot help but believe it. A man's character for truthfulness shows itself in every accent of his voice, and by this time, you must be very well aware that when I speak, I speak the truth."

Pauline moved from the mantelpiece and he loosed her arm.

"Well?" she said interrogatively.

She did not know it, but she was breathing very rapidly through her nose, and her charming nostrils were distended. Still, she probably noticed the admiration in Mr Jetsam's glance.

"Miss Dartmouth," he began, and then stopped.

Simultaneously they both thought of the invalid stretched moveless on the bed, and Pauline bent over that form. The eyes blinked irregularly, and always they stared up at the same point of the ceiling. They were dry, but Pauline noticed traces of tears on the rugged cheeks, and she wiped them away – it was her mission.

"Ah!" she murmured. "You can't advise me what I ought to do."

And then she faced Mr Jetsam once more, still standing by the bed. The table-lamp, with the crimson silk shade, and the bright fire gave sufficient light.

"Miss Dartmouth," Mr Jetsam recommenced, "a great crime was committed long ago in the Ilam family, one of the most cruel crimes conceivable. It can never be atoned for in full, or nearly in full; but, even now, after many, many years, it can be partially atoned for."

"Who committed this crime? and what was it? Murder?" gasped Pauline in a breath.

"I cannot be sure who committed it," replied the man; "and it was not murder. It was worse than murder."

"How do you know it was worse than murder? How does it concern you?"

"I was the victim," said the man quietly. And then he raised his voice and repeated: "I was the victim. I am the victim."

"Hush!" she warned him. "Not so loud."

He turned to the bed with a strange expression on his face.

"Why not so loud?" he demanded. "She can hear, even if we speak in a whisper. She has heard everything, and she can do nothing."

He spoke bitterly, and held a pointing finger at the old woman. And her eyes remained ever fixed, blinking irregularly, regardless of the two beings near her.

"You are cruel," said Pauline. "You torture her."

"Far from being cruel," said Mr Jetsam, "I am kind. Justice is always kind, for it alone produces peace, and peace alone produces happiness."

"You would not talk like that if you had ever been happy," said Pauline.

"If I have not been happy, it is because justice has been denied me. If this old woman and her son have never been happy it is because they have denied me justice. But justice may now be done, and you yourself may be the first instrument of it."

"Tell me how," said Pauline.

"You will be the blind instrument," he said.

"Tell me how," Pauline repeated.

"I have been watching a long time at that window," said the man, always with the utmost respect – "and what I saw convinces me that you know more of this affair than you care to seem to know."

"What do you mean?" demanded the girl defiantly.

"Well," said Mr Jetsam, "Mrs Ilam cannot talk, cannot give instructions of any kind. Yet I saw you take a particular box from off the chest of drawers, and hide it under the invalid's pillow. In order to hide it, you actually disturbed the invalid. You lifted her head to enable you to conceal the box in the bed beneath it. That is strange, Miss Dartmouth. But I have no desire to pry into your secrets. You are a friend of the family, nay more, a relative, and you had the right to do all that you have done. But let me tell you at once that I have come in search of precisely that box. I hoped to get it while everybody was asleep; but I was prepared for emergencies. If your cousin Ilam had been here in your place I should have obtained possession of it without asking his leave. But you – well, I humbly ask you to give it to me."

Pauline gazed at the poor organism on the bed.

"Is he to have the box?" she asked. "Is he to have the box, Mrs Ilam?"

The staring, sad eyes did not move. There was not the slightest flutter of the lids.

"Why do you put questions to her?" asked Mr Jetsam moodily.

"She means that you are not to have the box," said Pauline, and then she addressed Mrs Ilam anew. "You mean that he is to go away without the box?"

The eyelids wavered and then blinked rapidly.

"That means ' Yes.' You must now go – at once. I have listened to you too long," said Pauline.

"It is impossible that you should refuse me," argued the man. "Impossible! I don't suppose that motion of the eyelids means anything, but even if it did, naturally she does not want me to have the box. Still, I must have it. Miss Dartmouth, everything depends on my obtaining that box. Its contents are essential to the bringing about of justice. I entreat you most urgently and most solemnly to give it to me. You cannot doubt my sincerity."

"I will admit frankly," answered Pauline, "that I do not doubt your sincerity. But, all the same, you cannot have that box – at least from my hands. It belongs to Mrs Ilam; she evidently treasures it highly. I put it under her pillow to satisfy her. Mrs Ilam is helpless, and I am in charge of her. You must go, I repeat – and at once. We have talked too much."

"Suppose I take it by force?" suggested the man.

"You would never dare," said Pauline angrily, and she rushed again to the bell. "If you attempt to take it I will ring the bell, and I will hold you till some one comes, even if I die for it."

"Mad creature!" he exclaimed acidly. "I could kill you. It is almost worth while; but I won't. You tell me to go, and I go; but my resources are not yet exhausted. Good-night. I can't leave without expressing the opinion that you've got both sense and grit, and plenty of both. But you've made a mistake to-night. Good-bye."

And while she stood with her hand on the bell-push Mr Jetsam passed very calmly out of the window, and the curtain fell in front of him and hid him.

It was the most curious adventure of Pauline's life, which, indeed, had hitherto been entirely free from the unusual and the mysterious. After a short period of hesitation she went to the window, drew aside the curtain boldly, and looked out into the night of the City. There was no sign of her late visitor, but the ladder rested against the balcony, a proof of his recent presence; otherwise, she might have persuaded herself that what she had been through was a dream. She shut the window and bolted it, and came back into the room. The old woman, with her dark burning eyes staring always at the same spot on the ceiling, seemed now somewhat easier. Pauline gazed at her, and, after having stirred the fire, lay down again on the couch.

And as she closed her eyes, the strange enigma of Mrs Ilam and her son and the nocturnal visitant filled her mind with distracting and futile thoughts. Who was this grey-haired man, at once so masterful, so dignified, and so desperate? What could be the justice that he demanded? what the contents of the lacquered box? She would have a real good talk with Rosie in the morning. That prospect comforted her. Rosie – Rosie – Suddenly she started and gradually she perceived that she had been asleep a long time – two hours, perhaps – and that something, some presence, had wakened her. Looking round, she noticed that the door, which had been closed, was now open.

She jumped up and went out of the room to the passage, but she could neither see nor hear anything. Then, as her eyes became accustomed to the obscurity, she detected a very faint, thin pencil of light at the other end of the passage, and on approaching it she found that it came from her sister's room. She crept forward, pushed open the door and went in. Rosie, fully dressed, was sitting on a chair near the window, which was not quite closed, and her face was hidden in her hands, and she appeared to be crying.

"Rosie," exclaimed Pauline, "whatever's the matter? Why aren't you in bed and asleep?"

And Rosie subsided into her sister's arms, weeping violently.

"I haven't been to bed at all," she said at last. "I've never slept in a room with a balcony before, and I couldn't resist going out on to this balcony to see how beautiful the night was. And I began to think what a splendid time we were having, and I watched the stars, and I heard the clock strike in" the tower over there, and the gardens looked so beautiful in the starlight, and a long, long time must have passed. And then I saw a man standing under my window. He was a man dressed in blue, with grey hair, and he began to talk to me."

"And why didn't you tell him to go away, my dear?"

"He seemed so sad, and he said such interesting things. Pauline, darling, there's something very, very wrong in this house – some mystery! He told me. No one could help believing what he says, and he has such a beautiful voice. I cried, almost, in listening to him."

"But who was he?"

"I think he must be some relative," said Rosie. "I think so. He didn't say. What he did say was that there was a black box which it was absolutely necessary he must have. Oh, Pauline, I'm sure he isn't a thief! He's a man who has suffered a great deal, and he asked me to get the box for him, and his face was so sad – well, I said I would. And he told me exactly where it was."

"Where did he say it was?"

"He said it was under Mrs Ilam's pillow; and it was true enough."

"How do you know?" cried Pauline, aghast.

"I crept into your room, and lifted Mrs Ilam's head, and took the box. You were fast asleep. He asked me to see if you were asleep, and, if you were, not to wake you. So I came as quietly as a mouse."

"And you obeyed him like that?" murmured Pauline, astounded.

"I couldn't help it. I felt so sorry for him. And his voice was so –"

"Rosie!" said Pauline. "You used to be sensible enough!"

"I couldn't help it!" moaned Rosie again.

18

An Arrangement for a Marriage

Juliette D'Avray had a small sitting-room of her own in the Carpentaria bungalow. It was on the first floor, and it looked west, whereas Carpentaria's study and bedroom both looked north, on the avenue. Three days after the affair of the black box, Carpentaria ran hastily up the stairs of his house and touched the knob of the door of Juliette's sitting-room, and then he drew back his hand, nervous and hesitant. He was evidently perturbed, and he pulled his fine beard in a series of quick twitches, and then he rapped smartly on the door and coughed.

"Juliette!" he cried. He was very much surprised to discover that he had not got complete control of his voice. It broke in the middle of his half-sister's name. "I must do better than this," he thought, trying to command himself.

There was a pause.

"Juliette!" he cried again, more firmly.

The word was scarcely out of his mouth when the door opened wide, and Juliette stood before him. They gazed at each other for a fraction of a second as if inimically.

"Why don't you come in, Carlos?" she murmured softly, and her eyes fell, "instead of knocking and making such a noise. What's the matter?"

109

Carpentaria was certainly astonished at the nature and tone of her remark. She seemed to wish to run away. Then he gathered himself together, with an immense show of force, as a man will when confronted by a woman who is helpless before him, but of whom he is afraid.

"I don't want to come in," he said. "Why?" she demanded. "You know why," he said.

"Indeed I don't," she asserted: and she laughed – a curt laugh.

"You promised me you wouldn't see Ilam again at present," said Carpentaria stoutly.

Juliette tossed ever so little her charming head, with its admirable coiffure. "I did," she admitted.

"Well," said Carpentaria, "he is at this moment in the sitting-room." Juliette's dainty nostrils began to dilate. "Carlos," she said disdainfully, "do you know what you are saying? To me! Mr Ilam is not here. I have already asked you to come in!"

"Yes," said Carpentaria, "but you don't make way for me. You keep well in the doorway, Juliette." She moved aside with a gesture of the finest feminine scorn.

"Is there space for you to enter?" she said, bitterly sarcastic.

Carpentaria stepped forward one pace. His foot was on the door-mat.

"Stop a moment, Carlos," she said warningly, lifting her arm. "I repeat that Mr Ilam is not here. I cannot imagine what put the idea into your head. But whatever put it in, let me advise you to put it out again at once. Under the circumstances, if you come into this room, now that I have distinctly told you that Mr Ilam is not here, it will be equivalent to calling me a liar. I could not suffer that, even for you, Carlos. I should leave you. We should quarrel for ever. Think what you are doing."

Tears stood in her eyes.

Carpentaria shuffled his feet in an agony of uncertainty.

"Come in if you doubt me," Juliette continued. "But if you do, it will be the end."

Carpentaria turned slowly away, and passed down the corridor.

"Of course I don't doubt you," he called out.

Juliette made no response. She waited till her half-brother had descended the stairs, then she shut the door quietly, and ran to the Louis Quinze sofa, with its gilded borders, that stood a little way from the window.

"You can come out," she whispered.

And from behind the sofa emerged the bulky form of Josephus Ilam.

"Great heavens!" he muttered, searching in his pocket for his handkerchief.

Juliette sat down on a chair and burst into tears. The contrast between their two handkerchiefs – Ilam's enormous, like himself, and Juliette's a fragment of lace no larger than a piece of bread-and-butter – was one of those trifles which put an edge of the comical on the tragic stuff of life.

"You are an astounding woman!" exclaimed Ilam, wiping his brow.

"I have lied to him – I have deceived him. You heard what I said?" whimpered Juliette.

"You behaved superbly," said Ilam.

"I behaved shamefully," said the woman. "But I did it for you!"

And she looked at him over her handkerchief, with wet eyelashes.

Ilam would have gone through unutterable torture for her in that moment. It was a highly strange thing – this late coming of love into the existence of Josephus Ilam. It transformed him. It made him feel that, at fifty, he was only just beginning to grasp the meaning of life. It made him see that hitherto his days and his years had been wasted on vain things, and that the only commodity really worth having in this world was such a look as Juliette gave him out of her impassioned eyes. He could not understand what so bewitching and lively a woman as Juliette could see in a heavy, gloomy fellow like him. For the matter of that, probably no other person, save only Juliette, could understand that mystery. But then, when a woman loves a man – she sees him in a radiance shed from her own soul, and it changes him.

"My poor friend," said Juliette, composing herself, "why do you put me in such an awkward position, coming upstairs like this, and in the middle of the day, too? You must have bribed one of the servants." "I did," said Ilam.

"Well, don't tell me which," Juliette put in quickly.

He bent down and kissed her. Yes, this heavy and rather creaky person, who had laughed at love for several decades, bent down and kissed a pretty woman sitting on a Louis Quinze sofa; moreover, he put his arms round her. He did it clumsily, of course, but Juliette did not think so.

"I was obliged to see you," he told her. "I couldn't do without seeing you. Why have you so persistently kept out of my way. You were so kind that morning – when Carpentaria surprised you. Has he been bullying you?"

"Ah!" exclaimed Juliette, suddenly excited. "I cannot tell you what he said to me. You know I love him best in the world – next to – you. But he said such things to me – such things!"

"What?"

"He said – oh, my dearest! – he said his life was not safe – he said no one's life was safe in this City – he said he had been shot at in the bandstand; and, you know, that business of the milk was dreadful. The strange thing is that Carlos won't consult the police about it."

"But how does this affect us – affect you and me?" demanded Ilam bravely.

"Dearest," said Juliette, "poor Carlos thinks – he actually thinks –"

"That I am trying to kill him?"

"He thinks you have something to do with it."

"But why? Why should I want to kill your brother – your brother?"

"Yes, indeed!" agreed Juliette. "And why should you want to kill anybody's brother?" she added.

"Of course," he said hastily. "Why should I want to kill any person at all?"

"Carlos says that he is not the only person you have tried to kill."

"Ha! And who is the other?. Give me the full catalogue."

"I don't know. He says you have buried a man in the grounds, and that he saw you do it."

"Juliette!" Ilam stepped backwards. Then he stopped. "Juliette," he repeated, "I swear to you most solemnly that I have never tried to kill any one." "Dearest, you shouldn't have said that!" she remonstrated. "You shouldn't have sworn to me. It is an insult to my love. Do you imagine that I believed Carlos for a single instant? Do you imagine it?"

She looked at him proudly, gloriously. "How splendid you are!" muttered Josephus Ilam, son of the soda-water manufacturer. The admiration was drawn out of him. He had not guessed that women could be so fine. And then he perceived that he, too, must be splendid, that he must be worthy of her; and so he proceeded: "Nevertheless, it is true that I did bury a man in the grounds a few nights ago." The perspiration stood afresh on his brow as he made the confession.

"You!" she murmured.

"I thought he was dead," said Ilam, speaking quickly. "I thought I should be accused of his murder. And so I – the fact is, I was mad. I was off my head. I must have been. Until yesterday I actually fancied I was being haunted by his ghost. Yes! me! me – thinking a thing like that! But I did ; and yesterday I was in that big crush, during the shower, in the Court of the Exposition Palace, and he, too, was in the crowd. I saw him, I touched him; he didn't see me, thank Heaven! Then I knew that what I had buried was not a corpse."

113

"Who is this man?" asked Juliette calmly. "My angel," said Ilam, driven to poetry by the stress of his emotion, "you mustn't inquire; there are some things I can't tell you – at least, not yet. When we are married, when matters are settled a bit, I will tell you everything, but not now."

"Why not now?" she persisted.

"Look here," he said, "if you persist I shall simply , go and kill myself."

She paused.

"My friend," she resumed, "you do not love me as much as I love you. The measure of love is trust, and you do not trust me completely."

"I love you in my way," said Ilam doggedly; "men are not like women."

"That is true," she admitted philosophically.

"I would tell everything if I was free to do so," he said.

"Dearest" – she addressed him in quite a new tone – "you know something about those attacks on Carlos' life."

She spoke with an air of absolute certainty.

"I have had nothing to do with them," he said.

"But you know something about them."

"Why do you think so?"

"I can tell from your manner," she said triumphantly.

"I know nothing for certain, nothing precise," said Ilam – "nothing that I can tell you – nothing that I dare tell you."

"Dearest," she remarked, with a faint acidity, "it seems to me that you have come here to-day in order not to tell me things."

He deprecated her tone with an appealing gesture.

"I can tell you, at any rate, -this," he said, "that your brother's life is no longer in danger – of that I am sure."

"You are atoning," she smiled.

"Which is more than can be said of my life," Ilam proceeded, not heeding her smile.

"Your life is in danger?" she questioned, rushing to him as though she would protect him.

Ilam, without a word, led her to the window, from the corner of which a glimpse of the avenue could be caught, and walking to and fro there in the avenue was the Soudanese.

"You see that man?" said Ilam. "It's the fellow they call' Spats' in the native village. I don't know why. He is devoted to me; he is fully armed; he follows me everywhere. I have only to blow this whistle" – and Ilam produced a whistle from his pocket.

"Darling" – and Juliette clung to him – "is it so bad as that? Who is it that threatens you?"

"The man that I buried," said Ilam quietly.

"But what are you going to do?"

"Well," said Ilam, "I'm come here to see you. We must get your brother on our side."

"I'll force him to understand at once," cried Juliette.

"No," said Ilam, "perhaps you would fail, as things are, but if you were my wife you would not fail then. Carpentaria, once the thing was done, would do everything in his power to protect your husband; he likes you well enough for that. He might be angry at first, but he would see reason."

"Dearest, you want me to marry you secretly?"

"I merely want you to go with me to the registry office at Putney."

"Is that what you came for?"

"That is what I came for."

"My love!" she murmured.

Yet, with that cold and penetrating insight which women have, she saw clearly that, though Ilam's idea of getting Carpentaria's assistance in a moment of grave danger was doubtless quite serious, it was also somewhat fanciful, and that Ilam's professed reason for their instant marriage was also fanciful, and was not a real reason, but only an excuse. He merely wanted to marry her at once, that was all, and although his life was threatened, he thought little of that. She loved him the more.

115

"I can make the arrangements pretty quick," said Ilam. "You will agree, my angel?"

And she nodded, and the compact was sealed.

They heard a scurrying in the passages of the house.

"Juliette! Juliette!"

It was Carpentaria's voice, and other voices mingled with it indistinctly – the voices of the servants.

"Yes!" she answered loudly and, whispering to Ilam, "Get out of the window; whistle softly for your Soudanese. You can get on to the roof of the outhouse. He will help you."

And noiselessly she opened the window, and Ilam, struck by her resourcefulness, passed out. She heard his low whistle, and then she ran to the door and into the passage.

"The house is on fire," said Carpentaria, meeting her.

"Is it?" she answered calmly. "Are the firemen come? where's the fire?" – She sniffed – "Yes," she said," I can smell it."

She was amazingly calm. "No. woman with a man concealed in her sitting-room," said Carpentaria to himself, "could behave so calmly upon being informed that the house was on fire. Her first thought would have been to secure the hidden man's safety." And Carpentaria ran downstairs with a great show of activity. He was baffled, disappointed, for he had deliberately set fire to his own house in order to drive Ilam from the sitting-room, where he felt sure Ilam was. And the trick had failed. After all, he had been mistaken. He had been convinced of his sister's deception, and lo! she had not deceived him. Carpentaria could have killed himself.

Happily the fire was of no importance, and it was extinguished before it had done more than about five pounds' worth of damage and alarmed more than about five thousand visitors to the City.

19

THE HEART OF THE CITY

The situation of the heart of the City was one of the secrets of the City. It was not located, perhaps, exactly where you might have expected it to be, and for a very good reason. The magnificent building which housed the managerial, clerical, and inspectorial staff of the City was near the south end of the Central Way. It comprised four floors, and more than a hundred clerks spent seven hours a day there. On the first floor was the President's Parlour, where Ilam held consultations with Carpentaria and with the heads of departments, from the department of catering to the department of road-cleaning. On the floor above was the Manager's and Musical Director's Parlour, where the august Carpentaria held consultations with Ilam and with the heads of other departments, from that of music, with its subsections (a) open-air bands, (&) theatre and other bands, (c) restaurant bands, (d) vocal music, (e) pianolas, gramophones, and mechanical orchestras, to the procession and fetes department. But the heart of the City was nowhere in this building.

There were also scattered about the immense grounds various other executive buildings of a smaller size, where sectional managers, viceroys of Ilam and Carpentaria, held their mimic sway. But the heart of the City was not in any of these, either.

Very few persons, even among those on the salary-list of the City, did know where the heart was; for it was not talked about. Talking about it was discouraged; the hearts of such places are never talked about. And it is a most singular thing that visitors to the City scarcely gave a thought to the question of the situation of the heart of the City. The most interesting of all the many secrets of the City seldom aroused public curiosity, so strange is the public.

The heart of the City, as I propose to reveal, was situated beneath the Storytellers' Hall, near the northern end of the Central Way, on your left hand as you passed from the north entrance gates. The Storytellers' Hall was an invention of Carpentaria's – one of his best. Between two o'clock and four, between five o'clock and seven, and between half-past eight and closing-time you could pay sixpence to go into the Storytellers' Hall and listen to a succession of American and Irish and English performers, whose sole business it was to sit in an arm-chair on the diminutive stage and tell funny stories. The entertainment consisted in nothing else. It was the simplest thing in the world, and yet one of the completest successes of the City. It was a success from the very first hour of its existence. The little hall was nearly always crowded, chiefly by men. One is bound to admit that women were not enchanted by it; either they laughed in the wrong places, or they turned to their husbands, sweethearts, uncles, nephews, at the end of the story, and asked if that really was the end of the story, and, if it was, would their husbands, sweethearts, uncles, nephews kindly explain the joke to them.

Well, the heart of the City was beneath that gay and mirthful structure. While storytellers told stories above the level of the ground, the most serious business of the City was being transacted a few feet away, below the level of the ground. Let me explain.

Take an average intelligent visitor to the City. He approaches, say, the northern entrance, and among the twenty patent turnstiles which confront him he chooses the nearest one that is empty. He puts a shilling on the iron table of the turnstile; an official in the livery of the City scrutinises the coin to make sure that it is what it pretends to be, and then pushes it down a little hole. The shilling disappears – not only from the sight, but from the thoughts of the visitor.

It is a highly remarkable fact – as he squeezes through the turnstile he actually forgets all about his shilling, forgets it for evermore!

Yet shillings are being poured in a continuous stream into the mouth of that turnstile and into the mouths of scores of similar turnstiles, all day. What becomes of them? Surely this question ought to interest the average intelligent visitor! What becomes of them? The turnstiles won't hold an unlimited number of shillings; nevertheless, shillings are falling into them eternally and they are never emptied; they are never even moved; they could not be moved, since they are imbedded in concrete. Here is a puzzle for the average intelligent visitor.

It will occur to any one that when four hundred thousand people have each paid a shilling entrance, quite a nice little lot of money mutt have accumulated somewhere in the City by nightfall; for, besides the entrance shillings, there is the vast expenditure of the visitors after they have entered.

The nice little bit of money runs to the heart of the City. That is what the heart of the City is for; that is why it is called the heart.

Now, the heart was a long, wide, and low apartment, lighted by electricity, and lined with concrete. In the centre, its top level with the floor, was a. huge safe, which by hydraulic power could be raised till its top was nearly level with the ceiling, and its doors bared to the persuasions of keys. Round about were large wooden tables, furnished with large and small balances, copper scoops, bags, and steel coffers. A few chairs completed the apparatus of the apartment.

The shillings of the clients of the City dropped through the mouths of the turnstiles right down to a small subterranean chamber, which could only be reached from a tunnel beneath each entrance. Thus, the officials in charge of the turnstiles had no control whatever over the coins once they had been slipped into the orifices. The coins were checked and collected by an entirely separate set of officials, who visited the underground chambers every three hours and brought back the booty, enclosed in coffers, in specially constructed insignificant-looking carriages, to the solitary door of the heart. And the door of the heart was by no means in the Central Way; it gave on a back entry running parallel to the Way and just wide enough to permit the passage of one carriage. The coffers were received, and receipted for, by an official of the heart, and handed by him into the interior. Neither he nor the collectors were ever allowed to enter the heart.

On the evening of the day of the secret interview between Juliette and Ilam, the inconspicuous door of the heart was guarded, not by its usual official, but by a tall Soudanese, and waiting close to him was an automobile with chauffeur on board. The automobile was one of several employed specially to transport the riches of the City to the head offices of the London and West-End Bank in King William Street. The journeys were made at night, twice a week, and the offices of the London and West-End were specially opened to receive the coin. Automobiles laden with vast wealth are less apt to be remarked when they travel at night.

Within the heart itself were three people – Ilam; a middle-aged man named Gloucester, who spent all his days in counting and weighing gold and silver, and who was the presiding genius of the heart; and, thirdly, a clerk from the London and West-End Bank.

Gloucester was weighing sovereigns, the clerk was counting coffers and piling them up in a corner near the door, and Ilam was idly inspecting the doors of the huge safe, which had been raised out of its well and stood open and empty.

During that day and the previous two days, what with a monster Y.M.C.A. fete then in progress, and what with the weather, over a million shillings had been taken at the turnstiles. Now, a new shilling weighs eighty-seven grains, and about seven thousand average current shillings go to the hundredweight. A million shillings, or fifty thousand pounds in silver will weigh, therefore, something like seven tons. Nearly the whole of this treasure had already started on its way to the famous vaults of the London and West-End Bank; only a few coffers remained. But there was, in addition, about ten thousand pounds in gold, which weighed about a couple of hundredweight, and it was chiefly for this gold that the last automobile was waiting.

"Seven coffers of silver, Mr Gloucester," said the clerk; "two of gold."

"I shall be ready with the others in a few minutes," replied Mr Gloucester.

"Then I'll be making out the check-sheets," said the clerk.

"Do so," said Mr Gloucester, who was a formal old person, and wore steel-rimmed spectacles. And he continued his weighing of the gold.

At this interesting and dazzling juncture, the unique door of the apartment, an affair of solid Bessemer steel, swung slowly on its hinges, and disclosed the figure of a man in a blue suit, with grey hair under his soft hat. Mr Gloucester, being just a little shortsighted and just a little hard of hearing, neither saw nor heard the visitor. Nor did Mr Ilam, who was actually within the safe, measuring its shelves. But the bank-clerk, who was quite close to the door, most decidedly did see the man. And the clerk started, whether with fear, surprise, or mere nervousness, will probably never be known.

The man shut the door.

"What –" began the clerk.

121

"Go to the other end of the room," said the man commandingly.

"Mr Ilam!" the clerk called out respectfully, alarmed.

"Go to the other end of the room. "repeated the man.

The clerk perceived then that he had a revolver. Mr Gloucester also perceived the man and his revolver, and Mr Ilam came out of the safe rather like a jack out of a box.

20

WHAT JETSAM WANTED

"Hullo, Jos!" said the intruder in a light, careless, and rather scornful tone.

It was a stroke of genius on his part to address Mr Ilam as "Jos." That curt and familiar monosyllable, directed like a bullet at "the formidable Ilam, the august President of the City, made such an impression upon both Mr Gloucester and the L. and W.-E. Bank-clerk that they took no part whatever in the immediately subsequent proceedings. They were astounded into silence. They trembled lest lightning should descend and utterly destroy the intruder.

And Ilam himself was plainly at a loss. He was about to say to the intruder, "You have no right to speak to me in such a way," and to order him out of the place, when the ridiculousness of protesting and the futility of ordering presented themselves vividly to his mind.

Besides there was the revolver.

So Mr Ilam said merely, in a sort of pained surprise:

"Jetsam!"

"Exactly," said Jetsam.

And the imperturbable fellow, with his grey hair and his shabby suit and his weary eyes, nonchalantly sat down on the edge of one of the counting-tables, his legs dangling, and his body leaning forward.

ARNOLD BENNETT

The two employes were by this time convinced that the
new-comer must be either the Shah of Persia in disguise, or else
some extremely intimate and life-long-friend of Ilam's, perhaps
richer than Ilam himself. The bank-clerk knew by sight several
chairmen of banks who were quite as badly dressed as the man
on the table. Nevertheless, they did not carry revolvers. The
revolver was certainly rather disquieting. However, they bent to
their work, as though both eyes of the Recording Angel were
upon them.

Ilam closed the door of the safe.

"The doorkeeper let you pass?" he ventured. "No, not at all,"
replied jetsam.

"He isn't at his post?

"Not just at the moment. I've had him removed for a bit.
He'll doubtless return as soon as I've gone. I thought it would
be simpler to have my own doorkeeper."

"What did the Soudanese say, though?"

"Which Soudanese?"

"The Soudanese who is outside the door."

"Oh, him? He didn't say anything."

"This is a serious breach of rules for you to be here, you
know," said Ilam. "And I must ask you to g o."

"I really can't go just yet," said jetsam.

"What are you doing here?"

"Nothing," said 'Jetsam; "except nursing this revolver. I'm
going to do something soon."

Both the bank-clerk and Mr Gloucester looked up. They
even went so far as to glance at their employer for instructions;
but their employer seemed to avoid the eyes of the underlings.
Then Mr Gloucester spoke in a low tone to the clerk, and the
clerk replied, and some bags of gold were bundled into a coffer
and the coffer locked and double-locked, and the bank-clerk
murmured respectfully:

"These are the lot, sir. Shall I take them and go?" "Yes," said
Ilam.

124

"Will you help me?" said the clerk to Mr Gloucester.

"Yes," said Mr Gloucester.

And Mr Gloucester and the clerk each picked up several coffers.

"Good-night, sir," said the clerk.

"Good-night," said Ilam.

"Stop that!" Jetsam exclaimed, turning his head slowly behind him to follow the movements of the pair.

"I beg pardon?" murmured the clerk interrogatively.

"I thought I told you to go to the other end of the room," thundered jetsam.

"But Mr Ilam"

"Go to the other end of the room, up there at that corner," Jetsam commanded sternly, adding, "or I'll blow your idiotic brains out! Do you hear?"

The clerk was in love with a girl who lived with her mother in a pretty little semi-detached villa at Wey-bridge. He thought of her; he thought of all the evenings he had spent with her; he conjured her up in all her different dresses; he heard her voice in all its tones-and all this in the fraction of a second. Then he put down the boxes and discreetly betook himself to the corner indicated by Mr Jetsam, thinking obscurely and slangily that to be a bank-clerk was not all jam.

"And you, too!" ordered jetsam, raising a finger to Mr Gloucester.

Mr Gloucester was not in love with a charming young thing at Wey-bridge. He never had been in love; he had never lived with any one except himself and a bull-terrier; but he was fond of playing chess at night at Simpson's and he suddenly saw Simpson's and the chess-boards, and the foamy quart, and the bull-terrier lying under the table. Life and Simpson's seemed infinitely precious to him in those instants. And he put down his boxes and followed the bank-clerk to the suggested corner.

"I must really –" he began protestingly.

"Silence!" exploded Mr Jetsam; and there was silence.

You must picture the large, low room, with its concrete lining and its half-dozen sixteen candle-power electric lights burning in the ceiling; and underneath these lights the four men – Ilam leaning against the gigantic safe which rose out of the floor in the middle of the apartment; Jetsam still nonchalantly swinging his legs as he sat on the table, facing him directly; and the democracy, somewhat scared and undecided, in a corner. Jetsam had his back to the door, and since the two piles of coffers were near the door they were out of his field of vision.

Jetsam winked at Ilam – deliberately winked at him.

"Simple as a, b, c, isn't it?" he pleasantly remarked.

"What?" demanded Ilam.

"What I'm doing now – holding up a strong room and its staff."

"You'll suffer for this," said Ilam.

"That remains to be seen," was the reply. "I gravely doubt if I shall suffer for it. Up to now, what have I done? I have asked those gentlemen to go into a corner and not to indulge in desultory and disturbing conversation; and they have been good enough to humour my caprice; and I have winked at you, Jos. Is there anything illegal in winking at you? A few days ago you did more than wink at me – you nearly killed me!"

"I must go," said Ilam. "I have an appointment

He moved slightly.

"Let me advise you not to move," Jetsam warned him, raising the revolver an inch or so. "It mightn't be very good for your constitution. You must grasp the fact that you are being held up. A worn-out operation, you will say – a trick lacking in novelty! Yes; but one, nevertheless, based on the fundamental human instincts, and therefore pretty certain to succeed. Indeed, I am surprised how simple it is. You might fancy from my easy bearing that I had devoted a lifetime to holding people up. Not in the least. I have never held any one up before. And yet, how well I am succeeding ! The thing works like a charm ; merely because you can see in my eye that I mean to be obeyed."

"I suppose you want money?" said Ilam savagely.

"I don't want impudence!" retorted Jetsam. "Apologise, if you please, my friend!"

"What have I said?"

"It isn't what you said – it's your manner of saying it that was unworthy of you. You mean to apologise for wounding my feelings, don't you?" Jetsam smiled. "No, don't move; merely express your regret."

"I'm sorry," muttered Ilam.

"There – you see!" cried Jetsam to the men in the corner. "Let that be a lesson to you. And remember, that only great men like Mr Ilam have sufficient moral force, when they are in the wrong, to admit the fact. Well, Jos, I accept your apology in the cheerful and generous spirit in Which you offer it ; and I shall not deny that I do want money. That is part of what I came for."

"How much do you want?" asked Ilam.

"Well," said Jetsam. "How much have you got handy?"

Mr Ilam intimated that there was a small sum in gold.

"A thousand in gold?" queried Jetsam.

Ilam nodded.

"Probably more," Jetsam commented. "But a thousand will suffice me. If I need a fresh supply I can always come again, can't I? And besides, all that is yours is mine, eh?"

Ilam maintained silence.

"Eh?" repeated Jetsam persuasively.

"Yes," growled Ilam, and his eye caught the eye of the young bank-clerk by pure accident.

At that moment the young bank-clerk, fired by martial valour, a thirst for glory, and the thought of what a splendid thrilling tale he would have to tell to the charming young thing at Weybridge, sprang furiously forward in the direction of Jetsam.

"Stop!" said Jetsam, slipping off the table and facing the youth, revolver ready.

The youth hesitated for the fifth of a second.

"No," said the youth, and came on.

Jetsam fired almost point-blank at the hero's face, and the hero started back and sank to the ground. And there was a great hush in the room and a smell of powder and a little smoke. The youth lay still.

"Get up!" said Jetsam fiercely. "Get up, or I'll kick you up!"

And, strange to relate, the youth discovered the whereabouts of his limbs and got up, and returned to the corner.

"A singular example of what imagination will do!" commented Jetsam. "The first chamber of this revolver was loaded with blank. I expected to have to use it for theatrical effect, to begin with, and I was not wrong. Let me add that the other five chambers are most carefully loaded, and that I once earned my living in a music-hall by shooting the pips out of cards with this revolver." He then addressed Mr Gloucester. "Now, old man," he said, "how much gold is there in one of those boxes?"

"Two thousand five hundred!" answered Mr Gloucester politely.

"And it weighs?"

"About sixty pounds."

"It isn't worth while breaking into it," said Jetsam smoothly, looking at Ilam. "I'll take the lot. In our final settlement, it shall be brought into account." His glance shifted to Gloucester. "Thank you," he added, "for this information so courteously given."

"Perhaps you are satisfied now!" said Ilam. "Why don't you go? You think you won't get caught, but you will."

"Surely, you won't give me away, Jos!" protested Jetsam. "I'm convinced you won't; because, you see, if you begin to talk about me, I should probably begin to talk about you, and think how dreadful that would be."

"Keep it up! Keep it up!" said Ilam.

"Hence," Jetsam proceeded, ignoring the interruption, "I shall confidently rely on you to see that these excellent gentlemen here in the corner keep their elegant mouths shut. I shall rely on }'ou for that. You understand, gentlemen, Mr Ilam wishes you not to prattle, even in the privacy of your own homes."

"Are you going?" said Ilam doggedly.

"Yes," said Jetsam; "and so are you."

"Me!"

"Yes, you. The money is a mere incidental. What I came for was your distinguished self."

"I'm not coming with you. I haven't the slightest intention of coming with you."

"You may not have much intention, but you are coming," said the suave Jetsam. "Besides, who is going to carry this box outside for me? I can't carry the box and a revolver, too. Obviously Providence has designated precisely you to carry this box. Come."

"Not I!" Ilam defied him.

"Come!" repeated Jetsam. "I have a vehicle awaiting outside, and we shall see what we shall see."

"No!" insisted Ilam.

Mr Jetsam advanced two paces.

"Listen," said he angrily and yet calmly. "If you don't come, I'll shoot you where you stand. You ought to be able to perceive that I mean what I say."

Ilam's reply was a mute surrender. He dropped his eyes, and the next moment the two underlings had the spectacle of the corpulent Mr Ilam lifting a sixty-pound weight and struggling with it to the door, followed by the revolver and Mr Jetsam behind the revolver.

"Stop in the doorway a second," ordered Jetsam. He addressed the clerks again. "If I were you, I shouldn't hurry out of here. You might catch cold."

And then they saw Ilam disappear, the box in his arms, and Mr Jetsam follow him. Mr Jetsam closed the door. The clerks were alone.

"Well, of all the – !" exclaimed the younger man.

"I wonder how soon it will be safe for us to leave!" said Mr Gloucester.

21

INTERRUPTING A CONCERT

That evening the nightly concert of the "Carpentaria Band" was held in the great court of the Exposition Palace, partly because the weather was threatening, and partly because the Y.M.C.A. wished it so. The stalwart members of the Y.M.C.A. were prominent and joyous, and they pervaded the City to the number of some fifty thousand. They were nearly all young, and they were all, without exception, enthusiastic. They had taken possession of practically the whole of the tables on the three tiers of balconies that surrounded the court, and there was also a considerable sprinkling of them on the ground floor. They liked Carpentaria; they like his music; they liked his way of conducting. They admired him when he split the drums of their ears, and they equally admired him when he wooed those organs with a hint of sound that was something less than a whisper. They violently cheered his marches, and with the same violence they cheered his serenades and his cradle-songs.

Consequently Carpentaria was content. He was more than content – he glowed with pleasure. He was the centre of the vast illuminated court, with its ornate architecture, and its wonderful roof, and its serried rows of lights. All eyes were centred on him. He swayed not only his band, but the multitude, by a single movement of the slim baton – that magic bit of ivory which he held in his hand. He said to himself that he had never had a better, a more appreciative and enthusiastic audience in the whole of his glorious career. The result was, that he conducted in his most variegated and polychromatic manner. He did things with his wand that no conductor had ever done with a wand before; he performed gyrations, contortions, and acrobatics beyond all his previous exploits. In a word, he surpassed himself.

He was in the very act of surpassing himself, in his renowned "Cockney Serenade," when he observed, out of the tail of his eye, a middle-aged man, who was forcing his way at all costs across the floor of the hall towards the bandstand.

When seven thousand people are packed on chairs on a single floor, it is not' the quietest task in the world to penetrate through them. And the middle-aged man was not doing it quietly, in fact, he was making decidedly more noise than the "Cockney Serenade," and attracting quite as much attention.

A number of ardently musical young men on the grand balcony leaned over the wrought-iron parapet and advised the middle-aged man to lie down and die, in a manner unmistakably ferocious. (It is extraordinary how ferocious a youth can be on mere lemonade.) But the middle-aged man continued his course, and he arrived at the bandstand, despite official and unofficial protests, simultaneously with the conclusion of the serenade.

Gales of applause swept about the court, and Carpentaria bowed, and bowed again – bowed innumerably, all the time regarding the middle-aged man with angry and suppressed curiosity. The middle-aged man had lifted up a hand and pulled the triangle-player by the belt of his magnificent uniform, and the triangle-player had bent down to speak to him.

"What is it? What is it?" asked Carpentaria, his nerves on edge.

"A person insists on speaking to you, sir," replied the triangle-player.

"He cannot," snapped Carpentaria.

"He says he shall," said the triangle-player.

"I'll –" Carpentaria began an anathema, and then stopped. He went to the rail of the bandstand and leaned over to the middle-aged man.

"At your age," he said grimly, "you ought to know better than to interrupt my concerts in this way. Who are you? What do you want?"

"My name is Gloucester, sir," was the answer. "Doubtless you recollect."

"I do nothing of the kind," said Carpentaria.

"I'm in charge of the – er –" Here Gloucester stood up on tiptoe in an endeavour to whisper directly into Carpentaria's ear – "the strong-rooms."

"Well," asked Carpentaria, "what do you want?"

"Been robbed, sir."

"Great Heavens, man!" Carpentaria exploded. "You come to interrupt my concert because the strong-rooms have been robbed!"

"Two thousand five hundred pounds, sir."

"I don't care if it's two thousand times two thousand five hundred pounds. Go away! Go and worry Mr Ilam."

"That's just it, sir. Mr Ilam has been taken, too."

By this time the multitudinous eyes of the audience were fixed on Carpentaria and his interlocutor, and everybody was sapiently saying to everybody else that something extraordinary must have occurred.

"What do you mean – Mr Ilam been taken?" Carpentaria demanded.

"He's been carried off – he carried the money off – he was forced to, sir. Revolver, sir. Can't you come, sir?"

"Can I come? Ye gods! Man, do you know what a concert is? Can I come? Of course I can't come!"

"Mr Ilam may be dead, sir."

"We shall have leisure to bury him after the concert," said Carpentaria. "Go away. Go and consult Lapping, head of the police department. Or, rather, don't. You'll upset the audience making your way out. Sit down. Sit right down there, and don't move. We're going to play my new arrangement of the" Glory Song "with variations. You'll see it will bring the house down. It will be something you'll remember as long as you live."

"But, sir," pleaded Mr Gloucester pathetically.

"Sit down – and listen," Carpentaria repeated sternly.

He returned to the centre of his men. He rapped the magic wand on his desk, and-the next moment the band had burst deliriously into the now famous orchestral arrangement of the "Glory Song." The audience was thrilled by the waves of sound that emanated from the instruments, especially when the variations began. So the entertainment continued, while Mr Gloucester, consuming his middle-aged impatience as best he could, ruminated upon the strange caprices of employers. He had been an employe all his life; he had never commanded; and his conclusion, at the age of fifty odd, was to the effect that the nature of employers is incomprehensible, and that you never know what they will do next.

"Excuse me, sir." He timidly touched Carpentaria when the concert was over.

Carpentaria, it appeared, in the rush and fever of the music, had forgotten all about him, and was on the point of leaving the court deafened by applause.

"Ah, yes!" said Carpentaria. "That thief. Two thousand five hundred pounds. And you say that Mr Ilam has been carried off. Tell me all about that. Come this way. Come into the street – it is always the most private place."

And in the Central Way, near the fountain, upon which coloured lights were reflected from below, Mr Gloucester related in detail to Carpentaria the episode of the theft.

"You say it was a man dressed in blue, with grey hair?"

"Yes, sir."

"And there were three of you, including Mr Ilam, and you could not manage to disarm him?"

"It might have meant death for the first of us, sir."

"Well," said Carpentaria absently, "what if it did?"

Mr Gloucester grunted.

"You said I was to consult Mr Lapping, sir. Shall we go there?"

"No," said Carpentaria, "not yet. I will look into it myself first. The principal mystery is that of the doorkeeper. What is his name?"

"Wiggins."

"And he has disappeared?"

"He was not there when I left, sir. And he could not have been there when the thief entered."

"Why not?"

"Because he would not have allowed the thief to enter, sir. He has strict orders."

"Humph! Come along."

They hastened up the Central Way, in a northerly direction. The rain had kept off, and the illuminations, which were superb, evidently met with the ecstatic approval of the Y.M.C.A. adherents, who paraded to and fro, and filled the flying cars, with the hectic enjoyment of people who feel that closing time is near. The progress made by Carpentaria and his companion was therefore not of the quickest.

"It's more than an hour since," said Mr Gloucester, daring to show his discontent.

"What is?" asked Carpentaria.

"Since the crime occurred."

"The fellow must have calculated on my concert," replied Carpentaria. "He probably knew that everybody in this City runs to me when the slightest thing goes wrong."

"The slightest thing!" repeated Mr Gloucester bitterly – but not aloud, only in his secret soul.

They hurried round by the side of the Storytellers' Hall, and so to the passage at the back. And standing at the entrance to the vaults, underneath a solitary jet of electric light, was Wiggins, the doorkeeper of the heart of the City. He was a man aged about thirty-five, six feet two high, and not quite so broad.

"So you're here?" exclaimed Carpentaria.

"Yes, sir."

"Where have you been since – since Mr Ilam arrived here?"

"I did what you told me, sir," said Wiggins, with an air of independence. Wiggins was not a Mr Gloucester.

"What was that?" demanded Carpentaria mystified.

"Why, your note, sir."

"What note?"

Wiggins pulled a crumpled paper from his pocket and handed it to Carpentaria, who read:

"Come to me in my office at once. If I am not there, wait for me. The bearer will take your duties meanwhile.

C. CARPENTARIA."

"Oh!" said Carpentaria. "And who brought this?"

"A Soudanese, sir."

"Which Soudanese?"

"I don't know. They're all alike to me."

"And it didn't occur to you that this note was forged?"

"No, sir. Why should it?"

"It didn't occur to you," Carpentaria continued, "that I was conducting my concert, and that therefore I couldn't possibly be in my office?"

"I didn't know anything about any concert, sir. I'm doorkeeper here –"

"Not know about my concert!" cried Carpentaria. Then he calmed himself. "Mr Ilam came before the Soudanese brought this note to you?"

"Yes, sir, but only a few seconds before. He had but just gone in when the Soudanese came. I was talking to the driver of the motor-car as was waiting, sir, here in front of the door."

"Oh. So there was a motor-car?"

"Yes, sir. It was one of the City cars. No. 28, sir. To take the money away, sir."

"Good. Who was the driver? Do you know his name?"

"I think his name's Pratt, sir."

"Then you left immediately and went to my office and waited for me, and then?"

"Then I got tired of waiting and I came back here, sir."

"Good," said Carpentaria. "Mr Gloucester, the garage is indicated as our next resort."

The immense garage of the City was close to the northern entrance gates. And it, too, was guarded by a doorkeeper, hidden in a little box near the double-wooden doors.

"I want to know if Car No. 28 has come in," said Carpentaria.

"Yes, sir," was the reply. "Came in twenty minutes ago."

"Did you see it?"

"Yes, sir," said the doorkeeper.

"Who was driving it?"

"I didn't notice, sir."

"Show us the car, if you please."

They passed into the desert expanse of the garage, where a few men were cleaning cars. Car No. 28 was in its place. In shape it was rather like a police-van, but smaller. Carpentaria noticed that its wheels were very dirty.

"Open it," said he.

ARNOLD BENNETT

The key was found, and the interior of the car exposed to the light of a lantern. And at the extremity of the car could be seen a vague mass, a collection of limbs and clothes on the floor.

"Get in," said Carpentaria, "and see what that is."

The next moment two men were dragged out of the car in a state of stupor. One was the Soudanese entitled "Spats," who had become Ilam's bodyguard, and the other wore the uniform of an automobile driver.

"Who is this?" Carpentaria asked.

"It looks precious like Pratt, the man as usually drives this car, sir," answered the doorkeeper.

All the attendants in the place had now gathered round.

22

CARPENTARIA AS DETECTIVE

"You will now relate to me, as accurately as you can," said Carpentaria somewhat peremptorily to Pratt the chauffeur, "exactly what were the circumstances which led to your ceasing to be master of your car."

Carpentaria had had Pratt and the Soudanese carried to the strong-room, the heart of the City, where a chemist and Dr. Rivers had united to treat them for the effects of the narcotic which had evidently, by some means, been administered to them. Rivers repeated that, so far as he could judge, the narcotic employed was chloral hydrate, a drug more powerful than morphine, more effective in its action on the heart, and less annoying to other functional parts of the body. When Rivers and the chemist had finished their ministrations, Carpentaria had politely intimated to them that he did not absolutely insist on their remaining – a piece of information which surprised the doctor, who, having been let into one of his director's secrets, expected, with the confidence of youth, to be let into all of them. The three men, two white and one Ethiop, were thus alone together in the chamber.

"Well, sir," said Pratt, who was a fair man, talkative, with, just at present, a terrific sense of his own importance as the central hero of a mysterious drama. "It was like this: After I'd had the drink –"

"What drink?" demanded Carpentaria sharply.

"The drink the other driver offered to me, sir."

"What other driver?"

"There came up another driver, sir."

"In the City uniform?"

"Yes, sir."

"Who was he? What was his name?"

"No idea, sir. I seemed to remember his face, like, but I couldn't recollect his name. I asked him his name, and he said: ' Don't try to be funny, Pratt; you've had a drop too much.'"

"And had you?"

"Not I, sir – of course I hadn't. I'd made two journeys to the Bank with full loads, and the next one was to be the last, and –"

"And you hadn't had anything to drink at all?"

"Nothing to speak of, sir. A glass of port at Short's as I was coming back the first time, and a pint of beer – or it might have been a pint and a half – at the Redcliffe as I was coming back the second time."

"That was absolutely all?"

"Yes, sir, except a drop of whisky which was left in my flask."

"But how came the other driver to be in a position to offer you drink. Was he carrying casks and other things about with him?"

"No, sir, only a flask. Every chauffeur has a flask. Necessary, sir. Cold work, sir. And you'll recollect it hasn't been exactly sultry to-night."

"What did he say? Are you in the habit of accepting drinks from men whose names you can't call to mind?"

"He was in the profession, sir, and in the uniform; besides, he said he'd got a new cordial, fresh from Madeira, that would keep any one warm, even in the depth of winter, for at least two hours."

"But this isn't the depth of winter."

"No, sir; but, as the cordial was handy, I thought I might as well try it."

"And when you had tried it?"

"I felt rather jolly, sir. I never felt better in my life, and thinks I to myself: ' I'd better write down the name and address of this cordial before I forget it.' So I says: ' What's-your-name,' I says, meaning the other driver,' what's the name and address of this cordial, before I forget it? ' And I was just taking a pencil out of my pocket to write it down when I felt a bit less jolly and the pencil wouldn't stop in my hand."

"You were on your driving seat?"

"Yes, sir."

"And that is all you remember?"

"Yes, sir. Except that once, dreamy like, I thought I was in prison for exceeding the legal limit, and that all the lights in the prison were turned out, and an earthquake was going on."

"The other driver stood in the road by the car, eh?"

"Yes, sir."

"How was he dressed?"

"I've told you, sir. This uniform. Blue and white cap, same as this, and long overcoat."

"You couldn't see what he wore underneath the overcoat?"

"No, sir."

"And you?" Carpentaria turned swiftly on the Soudanese. "Did you drink too?"

"Yes, sah."

Spats smiled.

"And after you had drunk?"

Spats shook his head, still smiling.

"You remember nothing?"

"Yes, sah."

"What?"

"He means he doesn't remember anything," Pratt explained.

"You mean you remember nothing?" Carpentaria questioned. "Yes, sah."

141

"Why did you drink?" "Yes, sah."

The Soudanese looked at Pratt, smiling. "Because Pratt drank?" " Yes, sah."

"You have been waiting on Mr Ilam lately, haven't you?" "Yes, sah."

"When he came to the outer door there, and entered in here, did he tell you to wait outside?" "Yes, sah."

"You can both go," said Carpentaria. "Come to me at eight o'clock to-morrow, Pratt, in case I should want you."

"Yes, sir," said Pratt. "Yes, sah," said the Soudanese. "No, not you," Carpentaria explained. "Yes, sah."

"One moment," said Carpentaria to the Ethiopian. "Did Mr Ilam or any other person give you a note to hand to the doorkeeper outside there?"

The Soudanese shook his fierce and yet amiable head.

"What!" cried Pratt, addressing him in surprise, "didn't you come up and give a note to Wiggins and then go away again, and return a second time?" The Soudanese shook his head once more.

"Then there must have been two of "em, sir," said Pratt to Carpentaria. "This chap's honest enough."

"Me have brother," said the Soudanese, "same me."

"Where is your brother?"

The Soudanese shook his head.

"In the native village?"

"Yes, sah."

"Go and fetch him," ordered Carpentaria.

And the next moment he was alone in the great chamber, and he felt tempted simply to go to the regular police, of whom a few were constantly employed by the City, and tell them what had happened, and leave the whole affair entirely in their hands. And then the strange attraction which always emanates from a mystery appealed to him so strongly that he determined to probe a little further into the peculiar matter of Ilam's disappearance, without the aid of professional detectives. He didn't imagine for an instant that Ilam was dead. He was capable of believing that Ilam had disappeared willingly; and yet such a theory, having regard to the recitals of Mr Gloucester and of the bank-clerk (by this time doubtless on his way to Weybridge, and the young thing), was to say the least exceedingly improbable.

He unlocked the door and went outside. Wiggins was at his post, actuated by the exaggerated alertness which characterises one who has been caught napping.

"Anything happened, Wiggins?"

"No, sir. Nothing whatever."

"I shall return soon. If the Soudanese comes, keep him."

"Yes, sir."

He passed into the Central Way, which was almost deserted. The last visitor, the very last stalwart of the Y.M.C.A., had departed, and the sole signs of life in the great thoroughfare were a lamplighter extinguishing the gas-lamps which were provided in case of a sudden failure of electricity, and a road-sweeper in charge of a complicated machine with two horses. The clock in the tower of the Exposition Palace showed half-an-hour after closing time. The moon was peeping over the eastern roofs.

Carpentaria went to the garage, and, not without difficulty, for it was shut up, made his way into the interior and procured some light. He wished to make a thorough examination of the car which had been employed as the instrument of the plot. He had it drawn out to the centre of the garage, under the full flare of an electric chandelier. A sleepy attendant hovered in the background.

"Get a ladder and see if there's anything on the roof of the van – any tyres or boxes or anything," said Carpentaria.

"There's only this, sir," replied the attendant when he had climbed up, and he produced a cap and overcoat of the City uniform.

"Well, I'm – !" exclaimed Carpentaria, and a notion struck him.

"Doorkeeper gone to bed?" he queried. "Yes, sir."

"Wake him and tell him I want him." While waiting for the doorkeeper, Carpentaria scrutinised attentively the wheels of the vehicle; those wheels, even on his first visit, had put an idea into his head. Then the doorkeeper arrived, not quite as spruce and perfect as a doorkeeper ought to be.

"No one can enter this garage except under your observation?" Carpentaria asked him.

"No one," said the doorkeeper, positively.

"But you don't keep such a careful eye on the people who go out?"

"Naturally not, sir. They can't go out till they've been in, and if they've been in they're all right."

"Just so. Now try to remember. Soon after this car returned to the garage to-night, did any one leave the garage who was unfamiliar to you?"

"I don't remember, sir. You see, sir –"

"Exactly. I see. I am not blaming you. Your theory, though defective, is a natural one. Now, do you remember, for instance, a man in a blue suit, with grey hair, going out?"

"Upon my soul, I believe I do, sir."

"You are certain?"

"Oh no, sir. I'm not certain. But I have a sort of a hazy idea –"

"Look at these wheels," Carpentaria cut him short. "That's clayey mud, isn't it?"

"Yes, sir."

"Where could the car have been to get that?"

"There's that passage down under the embankment, sir, that way as leads to the river."

"Doorkeeper," said Carpentaria, "you are brilliant. I also have thought of that spot, where just such clay exists. But why should the car go down there?"

"Ah," said the doorkeeper. "There you beat me, sir."

"Then perhaps you are not so brilliant after all," said Carpentaria.

And having minutely examined the interior of the car, with no result, he left the garage, and returned to the strong-room.

The Soudanese was awaiting him at the door, and there were evident signs of a quarrelsome temper on the part of Wiggins. Wiggins had not forgotten the colour of the messenger who had handed him the forged note.

"Well?" Carpentaria asked of the Soudanese. "Where's your brother?"

The man shook his head, but not smilingly.

"Has he gone?"

"Yes, sah."

"No one knows at the village where he's gone?"

Spats shook his head.

"Wiggins," said Carpentaria. "Is this the man who brought you the note?"

Wiggins hesitated.

"No, sir," he said at length, resentfully. " But they're all alike, them folk are."

"H'm!" murmured Carpentaria. "Since there is nothing to guard here, you may as well go, Wiggins. You, too, Spats."

Two minutes later he was crossing the Oriental Gardens in the direction of the Thames. And when he had travelled two hundred yards or so he heard footsteps behind him, light, rapid, irregular. He turned quickly, his hand on the revolver in his pocket, to face his pursuer. His pursuer, however, was Pauline Dartmouth and no other. So he left the revolver where it was.

145

23

THE TALK IN THE GARDEN

She was so out of breath that at first it seemed as if she could not speak. He could hear her hurried breathing, almost like the catch of a sob, and in the moonlight he could see fairly clearly her flushed face, under the hat, and her tall, rather imperious figure. But he could not make out the expression of her eyes. Nevertheless, as he peered curiously into them, the thought suddenly struck him: " She is angry with me."

"Mr Carpentaria, I want to have a word with you," she said at length, stiffly.

"My dear Miss Dartmouth," he answered in his courtly and elaborate manner, "I shall be delighted. What can I do for you? I regret very much that you should have had to run after me like this."

"I've been following you up for quite a long time," she remarked, in a more friendly tone. It appeared as if his attitude and greeting had made some impression on her, in spite of herself. "First I went to your office. Then to the strong-rooms, then to the garage, then to the strong-rooms again, and now I'm here. I saw you crossing the gardens. Nobody seemed to be inclined to give me any information about you."

"No?" he murmured, in a cautious interrogative. "Now tell me; how can I be of service to you?"

She scanned his features. They were alone together in the midst of the immense gardens. A hundred yards away was the bandstand, the scene of the greatest triumphs of his life. And yet in that moment his triumphs seemed nothing to him as he stood under her gaze. Her personality affected him powerfully. He said to himself that no woman had ever looked at him like that. There was no admiration in her glance, no prejudice either for or against him; nothing but a candid and judicial inquiry. "I hope I shall come well out of this scrutiny," his thoughts ran. And the masculine desire formed obscurely in his breast to make this girl think favourably of him, to make her admire him, love him, worship him. He felt that to see love in these calm, courageous, independent eyes of hers would be a recompense and a reward for all he had suffered in the forty years of his existence. In a word she piqued him. He little knew that up to that very evening she had worshipped him afar off as women do worship their heroes. "Nobody ill, I hope," he ventured. She ignored the observation, and said: "Mr Carpentaria, what have you done with Cousin Ilam?"

"What?" he cried, amazed both by the question, and by the cold firmness with which it was put.

"I think you heard what I said," she replied. "What have you done with Cousin Ilam? Where is he?"

"Miss Dartmouth, do you imagine for one instant that I know where Mr Ilam is? I should only like to know where he is. I'm looking for him now. But I was not aware that the fact of his disappearance was known. Indeed, I meant it to be kept as secret as possible. I –"

"No, no," she interrupted him. "I was hoping you would be frank. I thought you had an honest face, Mr Carpentaria, and it is because of that that I have come – like this. I have just left your poor sister. She is in despair. She has told me all."

Carpentaria did not reply immediately. At last he repeated:

"Told you all? All what? You have soon become fast friends, you and Juliette."

"It is possible," said Pauline drily. "I have met your sister three times, but in seasons of distress we women are obliged to cling to each other. As for Miss D'Avray and me, we live next door to each other. What more natural than that I should call on her this evening? And finding her in a condition of – shall I say? – despair, what more natural than that I should ask her what was the matter, and what more natural, seeing that she has no women friends here, and is of a nature that demands sympathy, than that on the spur of the moment she should confide in me?"

"I assure you, Miss Dartmouth," said Carpentaria, "that I was entirely unaware of my sister's despair – as you call it. What precisely has she confided to you?"

"Why, about her engagement to Cousin Ilam, and your opposition."

"Pardon me, there has been no engagement," said Carpentaria.

"Pardon me," said Pauline, "there has been an engagement, because my cousin and your half-sister made it. Is there anybody better qualified than them to make an engagement?"

She lifted her chin.

"Well," said Carpentaria. "Let us assume that there was an engagement."

"They were to be married to-morrow," remarked Pauline calmly.

"To-morrow!" Carpentaria exclaimed, aghast. "Secretly?"

"Why do you pretend to be surprised? As for the secrecy, your opposition has forced them to secrecy, because your sister is afraid of you."

"And now that your cousin has disappeared, of course, they can't be married to-morrow," mused Carpentaria. "Hence this woe."

"Why have you taken such extreme measures, such cruel measures, such wicked measures?" asked Pauline, full of indignation. "I can understand well enough that you, as a great artist, cannot be expected to behave like other people; I can understand you doing mad things, original things. I can understand you defying the law, and taking the most serious risks on yourself. But I can't understand you being so cruel to your sister, and so utterly beside yourself, as to carry off Mr Ilam by force." Her cheeks had flushed. "By force?" murmured Carpentaria. Then he laughed loudly, violently, magnificently, after his manner. His laugh resounded through the deserted gardens.

"Juliette thinks I have removed her betrothed by force?" he queried.

"Naturally she does!" said Pauline. "The most extraordinary rumours are about. It is even said that you have had a quarrel and killed him."

"Tut-tut!" said Carpentaria! and after clearing his throat he proceeded: "Miss Dartmouth, will you kindly fix your eyes on mine. I tell you I have had nothing whatever to do with your cousin's disappearance, and that I was entirely unaware of his intention to marry Juliette to-morrow." She gazed at him doubtfully.

"On your honour?"

"No," he said proudly, "not on my honour. When I talk to a person as I am talking to you, if I say a thing is so, it is so. I decline to back my assertions with my honour."

"I believe you," she whispered softly, and her eyes fell.

"Thanks!" he said. "Will you shake hands?"

And she gave him her hand loyally. And he thought it was a very slim and thrilling hand to shake.

"Do you know," he said, "it was exceedingly naughty of you to go and credit me with being such a monster."

"Well," she replied, "perhaps I never did really believe it." She smiled at him courageously. "But I was angry with you for objecting to the match. I suppose you won't deny that you have objected to the match?"

"No," he said, "I shan't deny that."

149

"And your reasons?"

"I could not disclose them to Mr Ilam's cousin," he answered. "And perhaps they are not as strong as they were. I am beginning to think that just as you accused me wrongly, so I have accused your cousin wrongly. But I can assure you I had better reason than you. Ah, Miss Dartmouth," he added, "it may well occur that you will infinitely regret ever having come into the City."

"Never!" she said positively.

"That's very polite," he commented.

"We are getting away from the point," she remarked in a new tone. "I have left your sister in a pitiable state. If you have not had anything to do with the disappearance of Cousin Ilam, who has?"

"He may have disappeared voluntarily," said Carpentaria.

"Impossible!" she replied.

"I think so too," Carpentaria agreed. "At first I was capable of believing that he had played an enormous comedy in order to disappear in the most effective manner. But really the comedy grows too enormous to be any longer a comedy. It may be a tragedy by this time."

"And whom do they suspect?" queried Pauline impatiently.

"If I were you," was Carpentaria's strange response, "I should ask your sister, Miss Rosie."

"Rosie!"

"Rosie."

"Mr Carpentaria, what on earth do you mean?"

"I mean that your sister probably knows something of the affair. Where is she at the present moment?"

"She is watching Mrs Ilam, in place of the nurse."

"I gravely doubt it," said Carpentaria with firmness.

"But I have seen her there."

"It is conceivable," said Carpentaria. "But I gravely doubt if she is still there."

'' I shall be compelled to think that after all you are a little mad," Pauline observed coldly.

"We are all more or less mad," said Carpentaria. "Otherwise your sister, for instance, would not hold long conversations with a highly suspicious character every night from the window of her room."

Pauline, in the light of her knowledge of what had taken place in and about the Ilam bungalow on the first night of her residence there, could scarcely affect not to understand, at any rate partially, Carpentaria's allusion.

"I don't quite –" she began, lamely.

"Do you mean to say," he interrupted her at once, "do you mean to say, dear lady, that you are entirely unaware of the surreptitious visits of a certain mysterious person to Mr Ilam's house?"

"I am not entirely unaware of them," she said frankly. "I saw the man myself one night. I spoke to him. My sister also – also spoke to him. But I have not seen nor heard of him since. Nor has Rosie."

"Of that you are sure?"

"Yes, I think I may say I am sure."

"Then I must undeceive you," Carpentaria spoke firmly. "I also have acquired a certain curiosity as to that strange individual. And to satisfy my curiosity I have kept a considerable number of vigils. And I am in a position to state that, not only on the first night of your arrival, but every night your sister has had speech with that person from the window of her room."

"Who is he? What can he want?" demanded Pauline nervously.

"That is a question that I meant to put to you," said Carpentaria in reply.

"As for me, I know nothing."

"When you spoke to him, as you admit you did, did he not ask you to do something?" "Yes, and I refused his request."

"But your sister? What did she do?"

"Oh! Mr Carpentaria," murmured Pauline, "can I trust you?"

"You know that you can."

151

She related to him all the details of the episode of the black box.

"And after that," Carpentaria commented, "your sister continues to have stolen interviews with this man."

"I can't help thinking you are mistaken. Rosie would never keep such a secret from me."

"It will be very easy to throw some light on the matter," said Carpentaria. "Let us go to your house and see whether Miss Rosie is in Mrs Ilam's room as you imagine her to be, and as I imagine her not to be. I may tell you quite openly my opinion that Miss Rosie has had something to do with the disappearance of Mr Ilam. I am convinced, indeed I know, that he has been spirited away, together with a trifling amount of money, by our mysterious visitor, and since our mysterious visitor talks to Miss Rosie each night, she on her balcony and he beneath it – well, I leave the inference to yourself."

Pauline started back.

"Yes," she said, in a low voice, "let us go and see."

And they went, walking side by side in silence across the gardens.

"I will wait here," said Carpentaria, when they arrived at the side-door of the Ilam bungalow. "You can ascertain whether anything unusual has occurred in the house, and particularly if your sister is still at her post, and then you will be kind enough to come back and report to me. I will watch here."

Without replying Pauline passed into the house. In a few minutes she returned. Tears stood in her eyes.

"Well?" queried Carpentaria.

"Rosie is not in the house," she answered. "Mrs Ilam is alone. Happily she is asleep. Everything is quiet. But Rosie – !"

A sob escaped her.

PART THREE

JETSAM

24

THE BOAT

Carpentaria and Pauline continued to stand motionless outside the house, both of them hesitant, recoiling before the circumstances which faced them. The night remained clear, almost brilliant.

"The entire situation is changed," said Carpentaria at length. "A new factor has entered into it."

"What factor?" Pauline demanded.

"Why, your sister, of course!" he replied, with a slight smile that disclosed momentarily the quizzical male person in him. "Consider how it complicates the affair. If I had to deal only with the mysterious individual with grey hair and a blue suit – perhaps you do not know that he calls himself Jetsam? – I could go to work in a simple masculine fashion, and in the end one of us would suffer, probably he. But with a woman in the case –"

"How can you be sure," Pauline interrupted him, "that Rosie is in the case? "Can you doubt it?"

"I cannot understand why she should behave so!"

"Perhaps she knew him before," Carpentaria hazarded.

"Never," said Pauline positively – "never."

"Then he has certainly been able -to exercise a most remarkable influence over her."

"Not a hypnotic influence, or anything of that kind?"

"Perhaps an influence of quite another kind – quite another kind."

"But Rosie is scarcely half his age."

"Do these things depend on age?" cried Carpentaria. "They depend on glances, sympathies, and trifles even more subtle than sympathies. Besides, she is more than half his age."

"Oh," murmured Pauline, with a sudden wistful appeal in her voice, "I shall trust you to help me, Mr Carpentaria. Rosie may be in danger; she may be doing something very foolish, mixing herself up like this in the kidnapping of poor Cousin Ilam. What is to be done?"

"She is decidedly doing something very foolish," said Carpentaria, "foolish, that is, from a mere ordinary common-sense point of view. But I don't think she is in any danger. I don't think that either she or you are the sort of woman that gets into danger without very good cause. As to what is to be done, I have an idea. Mrs Ilam will be all right alone?"

"Yes; for a few hours, at any rate."

"Then you will come with me to the river? I have some investigations to make."

"Certainly," said Pauline.

And as they crossed the Oriental Gardens for the second time that night, he told her what he knew about the use, or rather the abuse, of the automobile.

The marble parapet of the immense terrace of the gardens stood a dozen feet above the level of high tide. The terrace was continuous from end to end, but in several places it formed a viaduct over paths that ran from the gardens at a steep slope down to the bed of the river. It was one of these paths, a specially clayey one, at the point where it ran under the terrace, that Carpentaria suspected the automobile of having taken. Assuming his suspicion to be correct, the automobile could only have descended to the Thames, and then, if the tide gave room, turned round and returned; or, if the tide did not give room, backed out without turning.

"Its sole purpose," said Carpentaria, as they talked the matter over, "could have been to pass something to a boat. Don't you think so?"

"Yes," Pauline agreed, and then she added, "unless they merely wanted to throw something into the river."

"What!" he cried; "a corpse?" "No," she said calmly. "I was thinking of the two thousand five hundred pounds in gold that you told me had been stolen." He paused.

"This is really very clever of you," he said. "But why should they throw it into the river?"

"Well," she said, "it's high tide, or rather it was, about an hour and a half ago. They might have sunk the money, intending to recover it at their leisure during the night when the tide sank."

"Yes, I must repeat," he said; "this is really very clever of you."

They were already beginning to descend the broadest of the three paths which led from the level of the gardens to the level of the river, and the wheel-marks of an automobile were clearly visible thereon, when Carpentaria halted.

"Suppose," he whispered, "they are there now?" "Who? Mr Jetsam and my sister?" "No, not your sister. Mr Jetsam and his – other accomplices – whoever they may be. I do not imagine that your sister has been concerned in the actual – er – affair. Indeed, she was at home with you at the time. But if Jetsam, for instance, should be down there now, alone or with others, there might be a row on my appearance. I will therefore ask you to stay where you are, Miss Dartmouth." She shook her head.

"I have begun," she said, "and I will go through with it. Besides, what danger could there be? People don't go shooting and killing promiscuously like that."

"Oh, don't they!" Carpentaria exclaimed. "Moreover, I have no fancy to be left alone here now," she added. "And most likely there isn't any one there at all."

"Hush!" said Carpentaria. "Can't you hear the splash of an oar? Listen!" They listened.

157

"Yes," she murmured. "And is not that the noise of a boat crunching on the beach?"

The path disappeared mysteriously before them under the terrace; they could not see the end of it. But the sound-waves came clearly enough through the little tunnel.

"We will go back," said Carpentaria, "and slip on to the terrace. Behind the parapet we can see anything that may happen to be going on. But quietly, quietly, dear lady."

In a few moments they were creeping across the broad terrace. Simultaneously they bent down, side by side, under the parapet and looked between its squat, rounded pillars at the water below.

Pauline gave a slight smothered cry, which Carpentaria, with an imperious gesture, bade her check. "Not a word," he whispered in her ear.

Rosie – Rosie and no other – was manoeuvring a boat off the shore. Her face, her dress, her hat, were plainly visible in the moonlight. She stood up in the boat, and by means of a boat-hook hooked to a large oblong stone, drew the boat to the shore. She then seized the painter and jumped lightly out. The curious thing was that she went directly to the large ; oblong stone, and with a great effort, lifted it up in her arms, tottered with it to the boat, and deposited it therein. Carpentaria perceived then that the stone was not a stone, but one of the coffers in which was kept the gold of the City of Pleasure. He perceived also that, attached to the coffer, was a dozen feet or so of rope with a cork float at the end. Rosie followed the coffer into the boat, pushed off, and then, at a distance of a few yards from the shore, pitched the coffer into the river. This done, she landed, made fast the painter of the boat to an iron ring in the wall of the embankment and departed; and she did it all rather neatly.

Immediately she had disappeared under the terrace, Pauline cried, starting up: "I must go to her – I must ask her what she means by doing such things."

"Pardon me," said Carpentaria; "you must do nothing of the kind. I most seriously beg you to do nothing of the kind. By interfering now you may spoil the coup which we may ultimately make."

"I don't quite comprehend you," Pauline observed.

"Miss Dartmouth," he addressed her excitedly, "there can be no doubt in your mind now that your sister is concerned in this plot, whatever it is. I am perfectly convinced that her motives are good, honorable, kind-hearted. But she is concerned in it. We must, therefore, so far as "we can, treat her as one of the conspirators –"

"But surely –"

"Always with profound respect," said Carpentaria.

"Had the person in the boat been any other than your sister, should we have revealed ourselves? Certainly not! We should have followed the plot to its next development, with this advantage – that we knew something which the conspirators imagined to be a secret. The fact that the person in the boat was your sister must not alter our course of conduct. And permit me to add, Miss Dartmouth, that you first approached me on behalf of *my* sister. We owe something to her, do we not?"

"Yes," said Pauline, in a low voice. "Then what do you mean to do next?"

"I suggest that we go back to your house, to see whether your sister has returned. May I ask whether, when you last spoke to her, she gave you to understand that she meant to stay with Mrs Ilam?"

Pauline breathed a reluctant affirmative.

"No hint that she was going out?"

"None. And –"

"And what?"

"Oh, dear!" Pauline sighed. "Must I tell you? Yes, I must! I'm sure Rosie is acting for the best, but really it was not her turn to watch Mrs Ilam to-night."

"Whose turn was it?"

"The nurse's."

"And your sister changed the rotation?"

"Yes. She said the nurse needed a holiday, and told her she could go away for twenty-four hours, and that she would take her place."

"What time was that?"

"About six o'clock this evening, I think."

"And where has the nurse gone?"

"The nurse has gone to a concert at Queen's Hall, and will sleep at the house of some friends at Islington."

"And does your sister imagine you to be in bed?" "I expect so," said Pauline.

They slowly returned to the neighbourhood of the bungalows. Carpentaria wanted to hurry, but it seemed as though Pauline was being held back by Some occult force. As a matter of fact, she dreaded the moment when she should re-enter the house. But at length they stood once again by the doorstep of Josephus Ilam.

"What am I to do?" Pauline demanded sadly.

"What do you think will be the best thing to do?"

"We have not seen your sister in the gardens,"
said Carpentaria. "She has most probably returned.
She would not be likely to leave Mrs Ilam for very
long, would she? Go and see if she has returned, if she
is in Mrs Ilam's room. And if she is, question her."

"But how? What am I to say? Am I to ask her if she has been out?"

"By no means!" said Carpentaria promptly. "You are to pretend that you know nothing. You must approach her diplomatically. Either she will tell the truth or she will –"

"Lie! Lie!" cried Pauline. "Say it openly! Say the word! Admit that you are persuading me to behave despicably to the creature who is dearest to me in all the world."

"If there is duplicity," Carpentaria answered, "you, at any rate, did not begin it. We are convinced of your sister's good intentions. What else matters? In a few days, perhaps to-morrow, all will be explained. Let me entreat you to go at once.. , I will await your report."

She shook her head sadly, opened the door with her latchkey, and was just about to shut it when Carpentaria stopped her.

"One moment," he said. "You have told me your sister believes you to be in bed." "I say ' probably.'"

"It is important that she should not be undeceived. I need not insist. You can easily make it appear that, having been awakened by some noise, you have woke up. Eh?" And he smiled.

She tried to smile in return, and disappeared from his view. Within the house, she crept upstairs, and into her bedroom, feeling like a thief. When she emerged therefrom she had put on a *peignoir*, and her *coiffure* was disarranged. She went to the door of Mrs Ilam's room, and listened intently. There was not a sound. If she was to obey Carpentaria she must enter, and she must wear a false mask to that sister to whom she had all her life been as sincere as it is possible for one human being to be to another. Well, she could not enter – she could not enter! Her legs would not carry her through the doorway. And so, instead of going in, she called : "Rosie!"

But her voice was so weak that she scarcely even heard it herself.

No reply came from the interior. And she called again, this time quite loudly:

"Rosie, dear!"

Then she opened the door an inch or two. There was a rush of skirts across the room, and Rosie appeared. She was evidently in a state of extreme excitement.

"What's the matter? Are you ill?" asked Rosie.

"I – I was awakened by some noise or other," said Pauline painfully, and it appeared to her that Carpentaria was whispering in her ear the words that she must say. "And – and – I – I thought perhaps something had gone wrong here."

161

"No," was Rosie's reply. "But how queer you if look, darling! You must have had a nightmare; You have quite startled me." Pauline did not answer at once. ; "You aren't undressed. You haven't lain down," ; she said at length. "I thought you could always sleep very well on that sofa."

"So I can," said Rosie. "But I've been reading. And besides – it's rather upsetting about Cousin Ilam. I wonder where he can be."

"Oh!" Pauline remarked summarily, "he's pretty •:,'• certain to turn up to-morrow. I expect he's gone 5 into town."

Rosie yawned. "Yes," she agreed.

"Well, good-night, darling," said Pauline, and took Rosie's hand. "Good-night."

"How cold your hand is!" Pauline observed, with an inward tremor. "Have you been out?" "Been out? What do you mean?" "Outside on to the balcony?" "No. I haven't stirred from my chair, darling. Bye-bye."

They stared at each other for an instant, each full of dissimulation, and yet also of love, and then they kissed one another passionately, and Pauline departed. They were women.

25

A WHOLESALE DEPARTURE

Having retired to her bedroom and divested herself of the deceitful peignoir, Pauline made her way, with all the precautions of secrecy, downstairs again, and so to the door which gave on the avenue. Carpentaria was not in view when she timorously put her head out of the door, and she was in a mind to rush back to her sister in order to confide in her absolutely, and to demand in return her entire confidence. She allowed herself to suspect for a brief instant that, after all, Carpentaria had not been behaving openly with her; but just then the musician arrived – he had evidently been watching the other side of the house.

"You were right," she whispered, before he had time to ask a question. .

"Your sister denies that she has been out?"

Pauline nodded.

"Does this help us?" she inquired, as it were, bitterly. "Are we any better off, now that I have lied to Rosie, and forced Rosie to lie to me?"

"I think so," he said.

"I don't," Pauline retorted. "And I have passed the most dreadful five minutes of all my life."

She seemed to be desolated, to be filled with grief.

"I'm so sorry, so very sorry," he murmured.

"No, no," she said quickly. "You have been quite right. We find ourselves in the centre of a mystery, and I have no excuse for being sentimental.

My trust in Rosie remains what it always was. Still, facts are facts, and I am ready to do whatever you instruct me to do."

"Well," he said, "your sister must have had some reason for insisting on watching Mrs Ilam out-of her turn; and that reason is not connected with the little matter of the boat. If she had merely wished to go unobserved to the boat she would have gone to bed as usual and said nothing, wouldn't she?"

Pauline nodded.

"It is obvious, therefore, that there is something else to be done, or to occur – probably in Mrs Ilam's bedroom. For if it is not to happen in Mrs Ilam's bedroom, why should your sister have voluntarily tied herself up there?"

"But what could possibly happen in Mrs Ilam's bedroom?" demanded Pauline, with a nervous start of apprehension.

"How do I know?" Carpentaria replied. "I can only point to certain indications which lead to certain conclusions. You will oblige me by watching, Miss Dartmouth."

"Where?"

"The landing and the stairs of your house. Is there a view of the stairs from your room?"

"Yes," said Pauline.

"Then you can watch from there." Do not burn a light."

"And if anything strange does occur?"

"Go to your balcony, and tie a white handkerchief to the railings."

"And you?" queried Pauline.

At that moment there was the sound of a window opening in Carpentaria's bungalow across the avenue, and a voice called plaintively:

"Carlos, is that you?" "It is I," he answered, as low as he could. "Go to her. Comfort her," Pauline enjoined him.

"I am coming to you," he obediently called in the direction of the window.

Both of them could see the vague figure of Juliette, framed in the window.

"Poor thing!" murmured Pauline. "Afterwards," said Carpentaria hurriedly, "I shall come out again and watch the outside of your house. With you inside and me outside, it will be very difficult for anything peculiar to occur without our knowledge."

And he left her, impressed by her common sense and her self-control, and withal her utter womanliness.

The hall of his own room was dark, and all the rooms of the ground-floor deserted. He mounted to the upper story. Juliette, hearing his footsteps, had come to the door of the study, from whose window she had hailed him, and she stared at him with a fixed and almost stony gaze as he approached. Her figure was silhouetted against the electric light in the study.

"Turn that light out instantly," he said with involuntary sternness.

She did not move, and, obsessed by the importance of giving to any one who might be spying the impression that all the occupants of the house had retired for the night, he pushed past her and turned off the switch.

"Oh, Carlos," Juliette sighed, "how cruel you are!"

He now saw her indistinctly in the deep gloom of the chamber, and her form seemed pathetic to him, and her sad, despairing voice even more pathetic. He went up to her impulsively and took her hand.

"Juliette," he said, "can you believe it of me?"

"Miss Dartmouth has spoken to you?" she asked, a glimmer of hope in her tone.

"Yes," he said. "Can you believe that I have – have caused anything to be done to Ilam?"

"Have you not?" she demanded eagerly.

And he told her what he had previously told Pauline.

She thanked him with an affectionate kiss.

'' Carlos," she said, and the words fell in a little torrent from her mouth, "I told you a falsehood this morning. I acted a part. He was in my sitting-room all the time. Can you forgive me?"

"I was sure of it," said Carpentaria calmly, "and I can forgive you," he added.

"You do not know what it is to love," she said. "You have never cared for any one – in that way. I hadn't – until I met –"

"Who says I don't know what it is to love!" he stopped her. "Perhaps I am learning. But tell me, when did you last see Ilam? Have you seen him since this morning?"

"Yes," she said.

"Where?"

"At his offices this evening."

"He gave no hint that he was in any danger?"

"No immediate danger. Oh, Carlos, he is not what you think him to be. He is an honest man, and I am so sorry for him, and I love' him. Where is he? What has happened to him?"

"I can't tell you now," was Carpentaria's reply, "but before morning we shall know more, or I am mistaken."

"It is for the crimes of others that he is suffering," said Juliette.

"He told you so?"

"No, but I guess; I am sure. I know all his faults – all of them. I do not hide one of them from myself. Why should I, since he loves me and I love him?"

"My child," said Carpentaria abruptly, "you might have trusted me more."

"I should have trusted you absolutely," answered Juliette, "but he is afraid of you. He would not let me. I could not disobey him. Sometime, somehow, you must have said something to frighten him, and, though he is so big and strong, he is timid; he has timid eyes. It was because of his eyes that I first began to like him. Carlos, what are you going to do?"

166

"I am going to watch," was the response. "A man came to the back-door not long since, and asked whether you were at home."

"A man came to the back-door?" repeated Carpentaria sharply, every nerve suddenly on the strain. "Who was it? What did you say to him?"

"At first I thought it was one of the night-staff, and then the man's face made me suspicious; I imagined it might be a thief – you know what a state I am in, Carlos – and so I told him you had just gone to bed, and I shut the door in his face. I didn't want him to think there were only women in the house. But, of course, it couldn't have been a burglar – here –"

"That is the wisest thing you have done this day, Juliette," Carpentaria remarked; and then he questioned her as to the appearance of the mysterious inquirer.

"Are you going to leave me?" cried Juliette, when Carpentaria picked up his hat, which had fallen from a chair to the floor.

"Yes," he said; "you must try to rest."

And then they were both startled by a strange noise on the window-pane. They listened. The noise was repeated.

"Is it rain?" asked Juliette.

"No," said Carpentaria, "it's gravel."

He went out on to the balcony. A form was discernible in the avenue below.

"Is that you, Miss Dartmouth?" he whispered.

"Yes," came the reply. " I – "

"Hush!" he warned her. "I'll be with you in a second."

With a brief explanation to Juliette, he hastened downstairs and let himself out of the house. Pauline was already standing at the door.

"Anything happened?" he questioned her.

"Nothing has happened," said Pauline, "but there is something extremely curious, all the same, in our house. It is a most singular thing that the housemaid, who never forgets anything, forgot just to-night to leave some milk in my room – a thing which I had specially reminded her to remember, so I rang the bell for her. There is a bell that communicates direct with her room – it used to be in Mrs Ilam's bedroom, but we have had it changed – there was no answer. I rang again. No answer. You know, I'm the sort of person that can't stand that sort of thing from servants, .so I went upstairs to her. She was not in her room. There are two beds in that room, the second one for the cook. Both beds were empty; they had neither of them been slept in. I went into the rooms of the other servants.

They are all empty. Rosie and I and Mrs Ilam are alone in the house."

Carpentaria paused.

"Did you tell your sister?"

"No, I came straight here."

"That was very discreet of you," said Carpentaria. "I am beginning to get frightened," Pauline added. "What can it mean? All the servants gone –"

26

THE EMPTY BEDROOM

Within the bungalow of the Ilams there remained only two persons who were legally entitled to be there, and those persons were Mrs Ilam, motionless for ever, but with her bright, tragic eyes staring continually at the same point in the ceiling, and Rosie Dartmouth. These two women, however, were decidedly not alone in the house. It was a large house, a bungalow more by the character of its architecture and its many balconies, than by its size and shape. Most bungalows are long and low; this one was long without being low. On the ground floor were the reception rooms and kitchen offices; on the first floor were the principal bedrooms; and above these was a low-ceiled floor of servants' bedrooms. Nor was that all; for the steeply-sloping roof had been utilised by an architect who hated to waste space as a miser hates to waste money, and hence, above even the servants' floor was a vast attic, serviceable for storage. The attic was reached by a little flight of stairs of its own, and it was lighted by two panes of glass let into the roof, one on either side.

The ground-floor and servants' floor were now dark and uninhabited. On the first floor the only occupied room was the bed-chamber of Mrs Ilam, where Rosie stood nervously by the mantelpiece in an attitude of uneasy expectation. The sole illumination was given by the small rose-shaded lamp, which

169

threw a circle of light on the white cloth of the invalid's night-table; all else, including Rosie, was in gloom.

Rosie was evidently listening – the door was ajar – and after a few moments she stepped hastily outside on to the landing, and glanced up the well of the staircase. At the summit of the staircase she saw the door of the great attic open, and a figure emerge; the figure, which was carrying a small electric lantern, carefully locked the door of the attic behind it, and then, with some deliberation, descended the narrow attic stairs, and, more quietly, the stairs from the servants' floor to the first floor.

The figure was that of Mr Jetsam, clothed in his eternal suit of blue serge.

The stairs and landing were quite dark, save for his lantern and the faint glimmer that came from Mrs Ilam's bedroom. Mr Jetsam had moved without a sound, for he was wearing thick felt slippers. He did not immediately notice Rosie on the landing, and when the light of his lantern caught and showed her dress, he started back slightly. Rose made no move.

"I did not expect you to be there," he whispered.

She regarded him with steady eyes, and then, without a word, motioned him to proceed further downstairs to the ground-floor.

"You want to talk to me?" he whispered again.

He had a voice which was curiously capable of being almost inaudible, and yet at the same time distinct.

She nodded.

He pointed to the open door of Mrs Ilam's room, but Rosie shook her head.

"Why not?" he demanded.

She shook her head once more, and they went downstairs to the dining-room, both silently creeping. With infinite precautions he opened the dining-room, and shut it when they had entered.

"It would have been better to remain upstairs," he said mildly. "The least possible movement is dangerous enough. At this stage a creaking stair might spoil the whole business."

"I cannot talk there," she said.

"But, since Mrs Ilam is utterly helpless," he protested, "what can it matter what she hears? She cannot talk."

"The fact that she hears is more than enough to upset me," said Rosie. "I am like that, you see. I know it is silly, but I can't help it. I wanted to tell you that I have just had a dreadful scene with Pauline."

"A dreadful scene! You've not quarrelled?" he demanded anxiously.

"Oh, no! But I've lied to her – I've lied to her in the most shocking way, and, what is worse, I fancy she didn't believe me."

"She suspects something?"

His tone sounded apprehensive in the gloom.

"I don't know; I hope not. In any case, what can she suspect? She's been in bed all the time."

"True," said Mr Jetsam reflectively. "True! You have behaved magnificently, Miss Rosie. Never, never, in this world, shall I be able to thank you. I had not thought that such a woman as you existed. You have given me the first sympathy I have ever had. Yes, the first! – without you I could never have succeeded. I could scarcely have begun. And now I shall succeed. Listen to me – I shall succeed! A wrong will be righted. Justice will be done. If it isn't, I shall kill myself."

He finished grimly, as it were, ferociously.

"Don't say that," pleaded Rosie.

He laughed. Then he lifted the little lantern and threw its ray on her face. She did not flinch.

"You are very pale," he remarked softly.

"What do you expect?" she answered. "You have gone much further – very much further than I ever dreamt of. You have led me on."

"No," he said, "it is your own kindness of heart, your sympathy with the unfortunate that has led you on. I assure you I was never so bold before I met you, before I appealed to you that night when you stood on your balcony. Do you regret? If you tell me to stop, to abandon my plans and depart – well, I will depart."

She smiled sadly.

"I do not want you to do that," she said. "Nevertheless, I tremble for what you have done."

"Do not tremble," he said coaxingly. "HI am not safe here, where am I safe? Is not this the very last place where any one would expect to find me and my – my booty?"

"But, then, sending the servants away," she exclaimed.

"Nothing simpler," he commented.

"I don't know how I did it," she mused, as if aghast at the memory of what she had achieved; "and as for to-morrow, how I shall explain it to Pauline I really can't imagine!"

"To-morrow," he said, "everything will be over one way or the other; you will be able to resume your habit of speaking the truth. By the way," he went on, in a tone carefully careless, "you managed to do what I asked you with the boat?"

"Yes," she replied.

"Did you meet any one?"

"Not a soul."

"And you pulled the plug out and cut the boat adrift?"

"Pulled the plug out and cut the boat adrift!" she repeated after him, amazed. "No; you never told me to do that!"

"Pardon me," he said, "that was the most important thing of all. It is essential that there should be no trace of the boat."

"I didn't understand," she faltered. "I'm so sorry. I never heard –"

"I regret I didn't make myself more clear," he remarked. "You see, at intervals during the night the watchmen do their patrols, and I know there is a regular inspection of the terrace. Supposing the boat is seen?"

"I really don't remember that you asked me to do that," she persisted.

"Anyhow," he said politely, "what you have done deserves all my praise and gratitude. But –"

"You would like me to go and sink the boat, wouldn't you?"

"I hesitate to ask you. It is really too much –"

"Yes, yes," she said passionately. "I will go and do it – alone." Then she paused. "But suppose I meet the patrol?"

"You are you," was Jetsam's response. "You are the President's cousin. You have the right to amuse yourself with a boat, at no matter what hour of the day or night."

"Just so," she admitted. "I will go now. I shall be back quite soon. Shall you be ready by the time I return?"

"Yes," he said.

"Everything is all right? "She seemed to question him anxiously.

"Quite all right," he said. "Let me thank you again."

With an impulsive movement he took her hand and kissed it. She blushed and trembled. Then he opened the door and they passed out into the hall.

"I will unfasten the front-door for you," he whispered. "I think I can do it more quietly than you. It may be left on the latch till you come back;" and he unfastened the front-door. Through its panes a faint light entered the hall.

"I must get my hat," she said.

They went upstairs.

"I'll leave you," he whispered. "You can manage?"

She nodded. He put the light on a bracket on the landing and ascended to the upper parts of the house. Rosie went into her bedroom. When she came out, wearing a hat, she noticed for the first time that the door of Pauline's bedroom was not shut. She pushed it open very carefully, and peered in. A female reflection of the moonlight redeemed it from absolute obscurity, and Rosie perceived that the bed was unoccupied, that it had not even been slept in. Instantly her mind became full of suspicions. Had Pauline lied to her as she had lied to Pauline? Was her part in the plot of Mr Jetsam discovered? No, impossible! And yet – Then she recollected having heard, or having thought that she had heard, the distant ringing of one of the service-bells in the house some time before Mr Jetsam came downstairs. She had forgotten to mention this disturbing fact to Mr Jetsam. Evidently he had not heard the ringing, or he would have questioned her about it. Supposing they were being watched, after all? And in any case where was Pauline? Pauline had given her to understand that she had retired to rest, and lo! the bed had not been touched! Full of tremors, she silently shut the door on the empty room.

She remembered Jetsam's threat of what he should do if his plans failed, and she hesitated.

27

THE PHOTOGRAPH

Mr Jertsam, having with an attentive ear heard the vague sound of the shutting of a door, came out a second time from the mysterious attic and descended the stairs. He was a man to omit no precautions, and every door that he passed he locked on the outside, not only on the servants' floor, but on the first floor. He penetrated then to the ground-floor, and fastened not merely every door, but every window. At last he arrived at the front door.

"It's a pity to lock her out," he murmured to himself; "but what can I do? It would be madness to let her assist at the scene I have to go through. She expects to, but I must disappoint her."

And he noiselessly bolted and locked the front door.

The fact was that Mr Jetsam's plans had been slightly deranged. He had hoped to get through his great scene – the scene to which all his efforts had tended – during Rosie's first absence on the river. He relied on Rosie; he had been amazed at her goodness and her fortitude; he had been still more amazed at his singular influence over her; and he naturally told her a great deal. But he did not tell her quite everything. He feared to frighten her. Hence proceeded one of his reasons for sending her to the boat, with the object of sinking the coffer further in the river as the tide fell. But she had despatched the business with such extraordinary celerity, and he, on his part, had been so hindered by such an unexpected contretemps, that she was back again before even he had begun.

Thus, he had been obliged to invent a new errand for her, and he flattered himself that he had invented the errand, and dispatched her on it, with a certain histrionic skill – and he had the right so to flatter himself. It desolated him to deceive her, to hoodwink her; but he saw no alternative.

Having secured the house, he ascended again, this time taking less care to maintain an absolute silence, to the first; floor. The affair was fully launched now, and no one could interrupt him. If Pauline awoke in her locked bedroom and heard things, so much the worse for her, he reflected. She could not go out on to her balcony because he had seen long ago to the fastening of the window. Therefore she might cry as much as she liked. He laughed as he thought of this, not having the least idea that he had so elaborately fastened the door and the window of an empty room.

He went into Mrs Ilam's bedroom with a slight swagger, and shut the door. A fire was burning in the grate. He cast a single glance at the bed and its mute and helpless occupant, and putting his little lantern on the mantelpiece, he walked round the room, inspecting its arrangement and its corners. Then, suddenly remembering his own burglarious exploit of forcing an entrance into the room by the window, he approached the window, flung it wide open and stepped outside on to the balcony. Far across the expanse of the Oriental Gardens, in the moonlight, he discerned a figure vaguely moving in the direction of the river. It was a woman's figure.

"There she is," he murmured. "Admirable creature! Why did I not meet such a woman when I was younger?"

Then he came in again, shut and fastened the window, and drew the heavy curtains across it, taking care that no chink was left through which light could be seen. Then he began to whistle softly, and he turned on all the electricity in the apartment; there were a cluster of lamps in the ceiling, and two lights over the dressing-table, besides the table-lamps, and his own trifling gleam of a lantern. The room was brilliantly, almost blindly, lit, and every object stood revealed.

He stepped towards the bed, and deliberately gazed into the eyes of the stricken old woman. Mrs Ilam's burning orbs blinked at intervals. Otherwise she gave no sign of volition or of life. Jetsam placed his eyes in the fixed line of her gaze, so that they were obliged to exchange a glance. She appeared to be unconscious of it. Only a scarcely perceptible tremulation ran along her arms, which lay stretched, as usual, outside the coverlet, like the arms of a corpse.

"Well," said Jetsam, "here I am at last, you see. Do you recognise me? I've changed, haven't I, old hag? But you can't be mistaken in me."

The pent-up bitterness of a lifetime escaped from him in the tones of his voice. But the old woman showed no symptom that the terrible past was thus revisiting her in its most awful form.

"You thought I was dead, didn't you?" Jetsam continued. "For over forty years you have been sure that I was dead, and that your crime was one of the thousands of crimes which go unpunished. And look here," he went on; "if you have any doubt, murderess, as to my identity, look at this. I'll make you look at it, by heaven!"

He bent down, drew up the trouser of his left leg to the knee, and pushed the sock into his boot, so that the calf of the leg was exposed. On the fleshy part of the calf could be plainly seen a large birth-stain. With the movement of an acrobat he raised that leg over the bed, over the eyes of Mrs Ilam, and held it there during several seconds. Then he dropped it.

"There!" he exclaimed. "That's to show you who it is you have to deal with."

His voice was cruel, icy, and inexorable. He had no pity, no trace of mercy, for the woman who, whatever the enormity of

177

her sins, was entitled to some respect by reason of her extreme age, her absolutely defenceless condition, and her suffering.

"They tell me you can answer 'yes' or 'no,' " he said, " by your eyelids. Blinking means 'yes,' and no movement means 'no.' I am going to put some questions to you. Did you take the photograph out of the box? Answer."

Mrs Ilam closed her eyes and kept them closed.

"What does that mean?" Jetsam grumbled. " Open your eyes again, murderess."

But Mrs Ilam did not open her eyes again. She obstinately kept them closed ; and she might have been asleep, except that now and then a tear exuded from under the lids.

"I'll make you open them," cried Jetsam.

His hand approached the old woman's eyes, but even his implacable and cruel bitterness recoiled from the coward villainy of touching that stricken and helpless organism. He drew back his hand, and some glimmering sense of the dreadfulness of the scene which he was acting reached his heart. The thought ran through his brain that it was a good thing Rosie had not been present.

"Very well," he said, "as you like. Only I know that you, or one of you, must have taken that photograph out of the box, and I have every reason to believe that it is in this room. In any case I mean to know very shortly whether it is or not."

So saying, he went abruptly out of the room, shutting the door, and climbed once more to the attic.

"Jake!" he called quietly.

And a Soudanese, the brother of Ilam's protector, "Spats," obediently appeared.

"I am ready," said Jetsam. "Come, pass in front of me. I will lock the door myself."

They went together to Mrs Ilam's bedroom.

"You know how to search, Jake?" Jetsam instructed him. "Everything in this room has to be searched to find a photograph – a photograph, you know – the same sort of thing as this." And he pointed to a portrait of Josephus Ilam that stood on the mantelpiece.

The Soudanese nodded.

"Begin with the chest of drawers," he said.

In a quarter of an hour the room was in such a state of havoc as might have resulted from the passage through it of a cyclone. Every drawer in every piece of furniture had been ransacked and emptied. The Soudanese had even climbed on a chair in order to inspect the top of the wardrobe, and had dislodged therefrom a pile of cardboard boxes. Every book had been torn to pieces. Piles of letters lay scattered about. The floor was heaped up with Mrs Ilam's private possessions. Chairs were overturned. One or two vases with narrow necks and wide bases had been smashed in order the better to search their interiors. The place was wrecked. But the mysterious photograph which Jetsam wanted had not been discovered. The Soudanese had found dozens of photographs, but not the right one.

The bed of the invalid was alone undisturbed. Among all the ruins of the chamber it remained untouched, white, apparently inviolate, and the old woman's arms lay ever in the same position, and her eyes, open and blazing now, gazed ever at the same spot in the ceiling.

"I have it!" exclaimed Jetsam suddenly. "The bed – the bed! The box was hidden under the bed, but I got it. The photograph is hidden under the bed, and I will get it."

He hesitated. Dare he search the bed? Dare he disturb its helpless burden? He wondered. He was ready for anything. He was capable of slaughter, but he wavered and retreated before the idea of searching for the photograph in the place where the box had been.

Then he suddenly decided.

"Take firm hold of the bed itself, not the mattress," he ordered the Soudanese, "and I will take hold on this side. Be very gentle. Do not disarrange the clothes. We will lift it over

the foot of the bedstead and place it on the floor. Carefully now
– carefully!"

And with the utmost delicacy the two men lifted the bed
bodily and laid it very gently on the floor, and Mrs Ilam's gaze
was directed to a new point of the ceiling.

"That will be a change for you," said Jetsam, with a touch of
compunction in his voice. "I was obliged to do it. We'll put you
back presently."

And he searched thoroughly the mattress and the bedstead,
but there was no photograph.

He paused and wiped his brow. The Soudanese stood at
attention by the side of the bed. Jetsam looked at Jake.

"Go and fetch him down," he said peremptorily to the
Soudanese. And Jake vanished.

"One way or another this shall end," he murmured, gazing at
the old woman in her lowly position among the heaped
confusion of the floor; and he waited, eyeing at intervals the
door.

At length the door opened, and the Soudanese came in, and
he was leading by the hand Josephus Ilam. Jetsam stepped
quickly behind them and shut and locked the door.

"Now then, Ilam," said he, "sit down. Make him sit down,
Jake."

And quite obediently Ilam sat down on a chair near the
night-table. He made no remark; he scarcely looked round; his
senses seemed to be dulled; it was as though his mind had
retired to some fastness from which it refused to emerge.

"What do you want?" Ilam demanded gloomily. "What have
you been doing?"

"I'm going to make one last appeal to you, Ilam," said Jetsam.
"I kidnapped you for this, I may tell you. I was determined to
confront the mother and the son, if necessity should arise. But
you nearly did for me by swallowing too much of that blessed
opiate. You are clumsy, even when you are a victim. However,
you've got over it nicely, haven't you? Pretty notion, wasn't it?"

he continued, "to conceal you in your own attic, where no one would ever think of looking for you. But it wanted doing, my weighty friend – it wanted doing."

"What are you after?" Ilam asked again, as if in the grip of one fixed idea. "You've got the money – what else do you want?"

"You know perfectly well what I want," said Jetsam. "My case is complete except for that photograph, and I've secured as much money as will keep me on my pins till I've forced you to see reason. But the photograph is lacking; you are aware of that. It's certainly rather hard lines on you that you should be forced to give up the very thing whose possession by me will ruin you. But what would you have? I am desperate, and no one knows better than you and this sad creature here that my cause is just. Tell me where the photograph is."

"I don't know what you mean," said Ilam doggedly.

Jetsam turned to Mrs Ilam.

"Listen, murderess," he said, and Ilam shuddered at that word: "if you do not answer my questions I will kill your son before your eyes. Does Ilam know where the photograph is?"

Once again the old woman obstinately shut her eyes and refused to give any indication.

Ilam, who seemed mentally to be quickly regaining his normal state, stood up and moved to the fireplace.

"Stand!" said Jetsam angrily, and he drew his revolver from his pocket. "I will know where that photograph is or I will hang for you. I shall not be the first man who has died in a good cause. Now, where is that photograph? Did you or your mother take it out of the box?"

He lifted the revolver.

"I took it out of the box," snarled Ilam – :" I – I – I – and my mother knew nothing."

"And where is it?" asked Jetsam, smiling triumphantly.

"It is here," Ilam cried, and he took a faded photograph from his breast pocket. "You never thought of searching me, eh? Ass!"

"Give it me," said jetsam quietly.

"No," said Ilam; and with a sudden movement he stuck it in the fire.

The flame destroyed it in an instant.

Jetsam sprang towards him, and then fell back as if stunned. Jetsam was beaten, after all. He gave a sort of groan and walked to the other side of the room, as if in a dream. He had failed, and he meant to commit suicide. All his trouble, all his risks, had gone for nothing. He raised the revolver again, and no one in the room quite guessed the tragedy that was preparing for them. His finger was on the trigger.

Immediately behind him was a draught-screen, and the draught-screen began mysteriously to sink forward. It lodged lightly on his shoulders. He turned, the revolver at his temple; and round the screen, from behind it, appeared Rosie.

"Don't do that," she said calmly, and she took the revolver out of his unresisting hand.

Jetsam turned round, saw that the person who had mysteriously interfered was Rosie herself, and sank down on a chair.

"You have done me an evil turn," he breathed, at the same time with a gesture ordering the Soudanese to leave the room.

"I have saved your life," she said simply.

"Yes," he replied, with a trace of bitterness. "That is what I mean. You are not the first who has saved my life. And if the first saviour had refrained we should all have been happier now."

"Do not say that," she whispered. "I –"

"You – you would never have met me," he said curtly.

"I am glad I have met you," she retorted, bravely facing him.

"Ah!" he sighed. "And yet you play tricks on me! Yet you make promises to me and break them!"

"No, no," she cried. "I only promised to go to the boat, and I would have gone to the boat afterwards."

"Why did you not go at once?"

She told him how she had gone by accident into Pauline's bedroom and found it empty, and how thus all her suspicions were aroused.

"I was afraid your plans might fail," she said; "and you had threatened to kill yourself if they failed; and I thought something dreadful might happen during my absence. And so – so – I hid myself here – without thinking. I'm so sorry."

And tears came to her eyes.

"A few minutes ago I might have been seriously perturbed by what you have told me," said Jetsam. "But what does it matter now? If your sister is against me, if the house is surrounded by spies, it makes no difference. I wanted to kill this man here. I should have killed him; but I thought of the annoyance it would give you. Yes," he smiled, "I did really. Not to mention the futile trouble it would cause me. And on the whole I regarded it as simpler and neater to kill myself. But you have stopped that. Will you oblige me by putting down that revolver. It is at full cock."

"You will not touch it?" she demanded.

"I will not touch it," he replied.

She laid it at the foot of the bed, and then bent down inquiringly to old Mrs Ilam, who rested with closed eyes.

"She is asleep," murmured Rosie.

"Through all this?"

"Yes, thank heaven! She sleeps very heavily sometimes. Will you not put the bed back in its place? I do not like to see it here. It is painful, very painful, in spite of all you have told me about her, to see this. She is very old and very helpless."

During the conversation Ilam had remained in a sort of stupor. It was as though the effort of putting the photograph in the fire, and then the shock of Rosie's sudden appearance, had exhausted the energies which he had managed with difficulty to collect as the results of the narcotic passed away; it was as though the narcotic had resumed its sway over him for a time. But now he came brusquely forward, taking two long steps across the room, and stood between Rosie and Jetsam, and he put his face quite close to Rosie's face, as an actor does to an actress on the stage.

"Are you this scoundrel's accomplice?" he asked hoarsely.

"Cousin," said Rosie, "Mr Jetsam is not a scoundrel, and I am nobody's accomplice."

"He has nearly killed me, and he has robbed me of two thousand five hundred pounds," pursued Ilam. "If that is not being a scoundrel, what is? Tell me that. You are his accomplice. You came into this house to serve his ends."

"Indeed, I did not," protested Rosie; "I came into this house with my sister at your urgent request."

"Yes," sneered Ilam. "That is what you made me believe, you chit! You worked it very well; but I know different now."

"Until I came here I had never seen Mr; Jetsam," said Rosie.

"You have come to understand each other remarkably well in quite a few days."

"Perhaps we have," admitted the girl. "But if you object you have a simple remedy."

"What is that?"

"You say he is a thief and almost a murderer. You say that I am his accomplice; we are criminals therefore. Bring us to justice. Have the entire affair thrashed out, Cousin Ilam."

"You know that I cannot do that," said Ilam.

"I am well aware that you dare not," said Rosie.

"The scandal would be intolerable. Think of Pauline's feelings."

"But suppose Pauline, too, is in the conspiracy?"

"There would always be the scandal. It would ruin the City."

"It is neither the scandal nor the City that you are thinking of, Cousin Ilam," said Rosie. "It is merely yourself or your mother. If it is your mother, well and good."

Ilam retired a couple of paces, uncertain what to say in reply, and possibly fearing some attack from Mr Jetsam, who stood behind him. There was a silence, and then Ilam murmured.

"Ah! my poor mother, sleeping there in the midst of all this!"

It was a cry from the strange man's heart, and another silence ensued. The situation had reached such a point as baffled all the parties to it to discover a solution.

It was Jetsam who broke the silence.

"I will leave you," he said in a low voice.

"Good-bye," he said, as no one replied.

"Where are you going to?" asked Rosie.

"I am merely going," answered Jetsam.

"But you will tell me where?" she insisted.

"It is vague," he replied. "Out of your life – that is all I can say. It was too much to hope that at the end of a career which has been one long and uninterrupted misfortune the sun of happiness should shine on me. I was destined to failure from the beginning. You do not know all my story; but you know some of it – enough to enable you, perhaps, to forgive me. Good-bye!"

He moved to the door.

"You will not leave me like that," said Rosie. "You dare not leave me like that. You are going to kill yourself."

"No," he said. "I have got over that caprice, I think. I shall drag out my existence to its natural end."

"Give me your address," Rosie said doggedly.

He shook his head.

"You are cruel," she whimpered. "After –"

She was interrupted by Ilam himself, who said:

"Rosie, go downstairs. I have two words to speak to this fellow. Go downstairs. Leave us."

His tone was cold and acid.

"Yes," Jetsam agreed after a moment. "Leave us; we have to speak to each other."

"You will not go without seeing me?" asked Rosie.

"I will not," replied Jetsam, and the next instant the two men were alone together in the room, save for the unconscious form of Mrs Ilam.

The door had been locked again, this time by Ilam.

"She is in love with you," Ilam shouted fiercely. "You have imposed on her; you have taken advantage of her ignorance of life, and she is in love with you! It is infamous. I am stronger than you, and unless you promise me –"

"Idiot!" Jetsam stopped him. "What are you raving about? You must be mad. You must have forgotten – as your mother forgets. As for this poor girl being in love with me –" He stopped with a hard laugh. "What has that to do with you?"

"It has everything to do with me," cried Ilam, and, as if transported by fury, he suddenly sprang on Jetsam, who was all unprepared, and, clasping him in a murderous embrace, threw him to the ground. "I've had enough of you," he ground out the words through his teeth. "And if I finish you, I can easily show that it was in self-defence."

And he had scarcely spoken when his hands fell lax in astonishment and alarm, for immediately outside the window, or so it seemed, there sounded four notes of a trombone, brazen, clear, and imposing in the night. No one who has heard Beethoven's greatest symphony will ever forget the four notes – commonly called the notes of fate – with which the most tremendous of musical compositions opens. It was these notes which the trombone had given forth. There was a silence, and the instrument repeated them, and in the next pause that followed, the two men who an instant before had been joined in a dreadful struggle, lay moveless, listening to their own breathing; and a third time the trombone sounded.

28

The Dead March

When Pauline, standing outside Carpentaria's bungalow, had communicated to Carpentaria the fateful fact that all Ilam's servants had disappeared from their rooms, and had given expression to the vague and terrible fear that was beginning to take possession of her, the musician said in reply:

"You have every reason to be afraid, and yet I shall ask you to try to calm your apprehensions. Whether the servants are there or not, nobody can get into your house without our knowing it, and when anybody starts to attempt to get in, there will be plenty of time for you to alarm yourself then."

"But Rosie alone there with poor Mrs Ilam!" sighed Pauline.

"Mrs Ilam can't do her any harm, at any rate," said Carpentaria comfortingly.

And with that he commenced a cautious perambulation of the exterior of Ilam's house, Pauline following him.

"I wish you would go to my sister until I have something to report," he murmured. "You will take cold, and you will work yourself up into a fever, and do no good to anybody."

"I shall not work myself up into a fever," replied Pauline firmly. "I am capable of being just as calm as you are yourself. Let us go at once into the house – let us go to Rosie."

"What!" expostulated Carpentaria, "and spoil whatever scheme is going on? No, my dear young lady, we have gone so

187

far that we must go a little further. We must catch the schemers red-handed. If we do not, our night's work will have been wasted."

The idea of weakly and pusillanimously changing a course of conduct at the very moment when that course promised the most interesting adventures shocked all the artist in him.

They stared blankly at the house, whose form was clearly revealed in the misty moonlight, but none of whose windows showed the slightest glimmer of light. It was an extremely modern tenement, and its architecture was in no way startlingly original; nevertheless, in those moments it seemed to both of them the strangest, the most mysterious, the most insubstantial house that the hand of man had ever raised.

Suddenly Pauline clutched his arm.

"I hear some one walking somewhere in the grounds," she said.

They both listened. In the stillness of the night regular steps sounded plainly from a distance.

"It is the patrol on the terrace," said Carpentaria. "It is assuredly on the terrace – the sound of heavy boots on stone flags, isn't it?"

"Yes," Pauline agreed, loosing his arm.

They were twenty or thirty yards from the house.

"I want you to be brave and to do something for me."

Carpentaria turned to her.

"What is it?"

"Go to the patrol, and tell him.,I have sent you, and that he is to remain within sight of the boat there, until further orders, keeping as much in the background as possible. Will you go?"

"Alone?"

"Alone. There is no danger. Besides, one of us must remain here, and one person can more easily keep out of sight than two. My fear is that the boat may be used again. The patrol is not to prevent the boat being used. He is not to show himself; he is merely to observe. You understand?"

"Then you insist on my going?"

"No, I entreat you to go."

And without more words she went. It was her figure, and not the figure of Rosie, that Mr Jetsam had seen in the gardens when he peeped out of the window of Mrs Ilam's bedroom.

Carpentaria, now alone, recommenced from a fresh spot his vigil over the closed house. He argued with himself with much ingenuity as to what point the persons who wished to enter it would choose for their appearance, but he could decide nothing. They might, he thought, come by the avenue, or round by the back from the other side of the buildings of the Central Way, or even through the gardens. He was growing impatient of a delay apparently interminable, and then his glance happened to wander upwards to the roof of the house. He could not see the roof itself, because he was now too near the wall, but it appeared to him that he detected a phenomenon above the roof which was somewhat unusual. He walked carefully away from the house until the expanse of roof became visible; and, indeed, he had not been mistaken. There was a radiance there. The small square pane of the attic, flat with the surface of the roof itself, was illuminated, and sent up a faint shaft of light into the sky.

Instantly he saw his own shortcomings as a counter-schemer against schemers. He had assumed that the schemers were not already in the house, whereas he had had no grounds for such an assumption. The schemers were most obviously in the house, and they had most obviously been there for a considerable time, since no one could have recently entered it without his knowledge. He was angry with the schemers, and he was more angry with himself, and one of those wild ideas seized him – one of those ideas which could only occur to a Carpentaria. He would catch these schemers himself, by his own devices, and he would do it leisurely, dramatically, and effectively. He would make such a capture as never had been made before. He did not know precisely who the schemers were, nor their numbers, nor their nefarious occupations in the house; and he did not care.

When once he was in the toils of a grand romantic idea he cared for nothing except the execution of it. He laughed with joy.

"Why do you laugh?" said a voice behind him.

It was Pauline, who had returned. She had given the instructions to the patrol.

"An idea," he replied – "a notion that appealed to me." And then he perceived that he must at all costs get rid of Pauline, and he continued: "My sister is extremely disturbed," he said. "Will you not, as a last favour, go and stay with her? Do not refuse me this. I will find some one to assist me in my work here – one of my trombone-players on whom I can rely. I – I really do not care for you to be out here like this. The strain is too much for you."

"But Rosie –" she objected again.

"Rosie is all right," he reassured her. "I will answer for Rosie's safely with my life; and when I say that, I mean it."

"I will do as you wish," said Pauline at length.

"Let me see you into the house," he murmured, enchanted.

He unlocked his front-door for her, and called out softly, "Juliette"

"Is that you, Carlos?" said a voice in the darkness at the top of the stairs.

"Yes," he said. "Here is Miss Dartmouth come to keep you company. Do not use a light – at least, use as little light as possible, until you hear some music."

"Hear some music? What music?" "Never mind what music. If you should hear some music you will know that you are at liberty to turn on all the lights you like. Miss Dartmouth will tell you why I want darkness at present. Here are the stairs, Miss Dartmouth. Cling to the rail. *Au revoir.*"

"But –" faltered Pauline. "*Au revoir*, I said," he whispered insistently. Before leaving the house he rushed into the kitchen, found a long clothes-line, of which he seemed to know exactly the whereabouts, and appropriated it.

The next minute he was tying the handle of Ilam's front-door firmly to the railing, so that it would be impossible to open the door from the inside. He secured in the same manner the side-door and also the gate in the wall of the kitchen yard. He then fixed pieces of ropes under windows, in such a manner that a person endeavouring to leap from a window to the ground would almost certainly be caught in the rope, and break a leg or an arm, if not a neck or so. "Cheerful for them!" he murmured maliciously. "I only hope it won't be Miss Rosie who tries to make her exit by the window. I have answered for her. However, I must take the risks."

He glanced finally round the house, throwing away some short unused pieces of rope, but keeping two long pieces. He surveyed the house with satisfaction.

"I think I can safely leave it for five minutes or so now," he said to himself; and he shut his penknife with a vicious snap and put it in his pocket.

Then he ran off at a great speed in the direction of the Central Way. At the southern end of the Central Way, nearly opposite to the general offices of the City, was an elegant building known as the band-house. Here dwelt the majority of the members of Carpentaria's world-renowned orchestra. Some members, being married to women instead of married to their art, had permission to possess domestic hearths in London and the suburbs, but these were few. The edifice was a very large one, as it had need to be. A peculiar feature of it was the rehearsal-room on the top floor, constructed, like the finest flats in New York, in such a manner as to be absolutely sound-proof.

Carpentaria rang the electric bell at the portals of the band-house, and the portals were presently opened by a sleepy person whose duty it was to admit bandsmen returning after late leave.

"Look 'ere," said the porter, "this is a bit thick, this is. Do you know as the hour is exactly –"

ARNOLD BENNETT

"Hold your tongue, you fool!" Carpentaria stopped him briefly, "and go and bring Mr Bruno to me at once; it's very important. Let's have some light."

"I beg pardon, sir," said the porter, astounded by this nocturnal apparition of the autocrat of the band.

"Mr Bruno is asleep, sir. He had two whiskies to make him sleep, and went to bed afore midnight, sir."

"I know he's asleep. Do you suppose I thought he was standing on his head waiting for the dawn?

Go and waken him – and quicker than that! Here, I'll go with you."

The two men went upstairs together, and Mr Bruno, principal trombone-player of the band, was soon sitting up in bed, awaking to the presence of his chief.

"Bruno, my lad," said Carpentaria, "give me your trombone."

"My trombone, sir?"

"Yes," said Carpentaria. "Mendelssohn once remarked that the trombone was an instrument too sacred to use often, but I think the supreme occasion has arrived for me to use it to-night."

"It's there, in the corner, sir," said Bruno, wondering vaguely what was this latest caprice of Carpentaria's.

Carpentaria rushed to the thing, took it out of its case, and put it to his mouth.

"H'm!" he murmured, after he had sounded a note gently. "I can do it, I think. Listen, Bruno! The occasion is not only supreme; it is unique. You are to rouse all the men; you are to dress, and take your instruments; and you are to go out quietly and surround the bungalow of our honoured President, Mr Josephus Ilam. You are to make no noise of any kind until you hear me give the first bars of a tune, either with my mouth or with this instrument. You are then to join in that tune." "What tune, sir?" "You will hear." "Where shall you be, sir?"

"You will see. Get up, now; don't lose a second." Carpentaria was off again. He returned to Ilam's house, and climbed to the

192

balcony of the window of Mrs Ilam's bedroom. It was fortunate that he had preserved the rope, for he could not have climbed with the trombone in his arms. His method was to leave the trombone on the ground, the rope tied to it; he kept the other end of the rope in his hand, and drew the trombone after him.

Then it was that he sounded on the trombone the terrible phrase of Beethoven's, which put a period to the struggle between Ilam and Jetsam.

He felt for the handle of the French window, and, finding the window fastened on the inside, adopted the simple device of leaning with his full weight against the window-frame. The whole thing gave way, and through a crashing of glass, a splintering of wood, and the tearing of curtains he backed into the room, the trombone held precariously in one hand and his revolver very firmly in the other.

The scene that confronted him was sufficiently surprising. Amid the extraordinary disorder of the chamber he found its three occupants all stretched on the floor. The old woman was apparently oblivious, but the two men, releasing each other, gazed at him for' all the world like two schoolboys caught in an act contrary to discipline.

"Did I startle you? I hope so," said Carpentaria, when he had found his bearings. "I meant to."

Jetsam was the first to rise.

"You with the red hair!" cried Jetsam. "You are trying to save my life again! "Never mind my red hair," said Carpentaria, ruffled. "I am not trying to save anybody's life. I'm here on a mission of inquiry. No one leaves this room until I have had a full explanation of everything. I have stood just about as much as I can stand of the mystery that has been hanging over this City for a week past. Ilam, let me beg you to get up and take a seat over there in that corner. Thanks!"

He relinquished the musical instrument as Ilam clumsily resumed his feet and obeyed.

"As for you, Mr Jetsam," continued Carpentaria, "you know, from accounts which have reached me, the precise moral effect of a loaded revolver such as I am now pointing at you. Go into the other corner." "I won't," said Jetsam. "You can fire if you like. As a matter of fact, you daren't."

"You propose to leave the room and defy me?" "I propose to leave the room." "Listen," said Carpentaria.

He took the trombone and blew on it loudly a few notes which neither Jetsam nor Ilam immediately recognised. But the musicians, who had by this time surrounded the house, recognised them. And at once there entered by the smashed window the solemn and moving strains of the Dead March in "Saul." The house seemed to be ringed in a circle of awful melody. Jetsam shuddered.

"Now kindly stay where you are," said Carpentaria. And Jetsam stayed where he was, at the foot of the bed, his back to Mrs Ilam's prone figure. The playing continued.

"What foolery is this?" demanded Ilam slowly. "It is part of a larger piece of foolery that has rescued you, Ilam," Carpentaria replied, and he was crossing the room to approach Ilam, when he saw something in the looking-glass over the mantelpiece, and he started back.

Mrs Ilam, the paralytic, roused in some strange way, either by the violence of the scenes at which she had assisted, or by the inexplicable influence of the music, was almost erect in her bed, and her trembling parchment hands had seized the revolver which Rosie had left on the floor, and she was endeavouring to point it between Jetsam's shoulders. The other two men turned and saw the fatal and appalling movement of the aged creature, who was evidently in the grip of some tremendously powerful instinct – the kind of instinct that only dies with death.

Carpentaria alone retained his self-possession. With a swift and yet gentle movement he disarmed the terrible old woman, and she sank back, with streaming eyes, helpless and moveless as before. The incident was over in a few seconds.

"And now," said Carpentaria, "I will hear your story, Mr Jetsam. But first, we must lift this bed back to its proper position."

"Very well," replied Jetsam, trembling in spite of himself. "You shall hear my story."

The music ceased.

29

MR JETSAM'S RECITAL

"We will go downstairs," said Carpentaria, when a certain amount of order had been restored to the room. "We shall be more at ease there."

"No," cried Jetsam, and there was a note of passion in his voice. "This old woman shall hear my tale. I tell it in her presence, or I tell it not at all."

Carpentaria gazed at Mrs Ilam's eyes, which made no response. Her bed was now replaced in its proper position, and those strange burning eyes perused their old spot in the ceiling. After the brief and terrible return of activity to that stricken body, it seemed to have sunk back into a condition of helplessness more absolute even than before. The eyes burned, but not quite with their former disturbing brilliance.

"Very well," Carpentaria agreed.

Ilam was already seated, apparently half-comatose. The other two men each seized a chair. And then there was a timid but insistent knocking.

"What is that?" demanded Carpentaria of Jetsam. "You ought to know; you have been master here for some hours."

"It is Miss Rosie, I imagine," Jetsam answered. "Your singular music has startled her."

Carpentaria walked rapidly to the door, unlocked it, and opened it. Rosie it indeed was who stood there.

"Ah, my dear young lady," he said lightly, without giving her an opportunity even to express her astonishment. "I would like you to go to your sister, who is in my house over the way. But I fear you cannot open any of the doors. Won't you retire and rest a little, after your complicated labours?" He smiled a little grimly. "Everything is all right here, and should your aged relative need your ministrations you may rely on me to call you. In the meantime, your cousin and I, and your particular friend Mr Jetsam, must have a chat on business matters."

He bowed, covering the aperture of the door with his body so that Rosie could not see inside the room. As for Rosie, she hesitated.

"I entreat you," he insisted, "go and rest, and don't have anything more to do with boats; you might drown yourself. And believe me when I say that nothing further will be done in secret. The moment I am free I will endeavour to free the doors."

Rosie moved reluctantly away from the landing. She had not spoken a word. Carpentaria closed the portal softly, and retired to his chair.

"You have my attention," he remarked significantly to Mr Jetsam.

"Well," said Jetsam, after a moment's pause. "It goes back a very long time, this affair does, Mr Carpentaria. It certainly began before you were born – down at Torquay. Torquay, according to what they tell me, was not the place then that it is now, not by a considerable distance; but it was fashionable. It had got a bit of a name as a good place to go and get fat in. Perhaps that was why a certain soda-water manufacturer went there to spend a year or so. He was a very wealthy man, and he rented a villa there. It's one of those villas on the top of the hill between Union Street and the sea, and it still exists. His age was about fifty, and he was supposed to be worth half a million or so – all made out of gas and splutter, you see. Being supposed to be worth half a million or so, of course he soon had the entire

197

population of Torquay knocking at his door and throwing cards into his card-basket. He made a wide circle of friends in rather less than no time, and being a simple, decent creature, though not faultless, he was pretty well pleased with himself. Now among the friends that he made was a certain widow, age uncertain – but in the neighbourhood of thirty, and her name was Kilmarnock."

At this time Mr Jetsam stood up, and bending over Mrs Ilam's bed with his smile so ruthlessly cruel, he repeated, staring at the invalid:

"Her name was Kilmarnock, wasn't it?"

Mrs Ilam made no sign. Mr Jetsam resumed his chair.

"A pretty woman, I believe she was, with magnificent black eyes; the most wonderful eyes in the West Country, people said," Mr Jetsam proceeded. "Husband dead some little time. Anyhow, she had gone out of mourning, and her dresses were the amazement of the town. They'd look pretty queer nowadays, I reckon, because that was before 1860. However, her dresses have got nothing to do with it, especially as the soda-water manufacturer – have I happened to mention that his name was Ilam? – especially as Mr Ilam couldn't see them very well. Mr Ilam was beginning to suffer from a cataract; both his eyes were affected, and the disease was making progress rapidly. You must remember that oculists didn't know as much about cataract then as they do now. Well, Mr Ilam was himself a widower – a widower with one child, age three years. He had been a widower for two years when he first met Mrs Kilmarnock. He liked Mrs Kilmarnock. She seemed to have in her the makings of a good nurse, and one of the things Mr Ilam wanted was a faithful, loving nurse. He was certainly in an awkward predicament. He also wanted a mother for his child; and Mrs Kilmarnock took a tremendous fancy to the child – a simply tremendous fancy. He was a man who talked pretty freely and openly, Mr Ilam was, and he made no secret of the fact that, though he preferred to marry a widow, he would never permit himself to marry a widow who had children of her own. And one day he said to Mrs Kilmarnock that, since he had never heard her mention a child, he assumed that she had no children.

"She replied that his assumption was correct, and that she continually regretted being childless, as she adored children, and felt very severely the need of something to give her a real interest in life. A month later Mr Ilam asked Mrs Kilmarnock to marry him, and she consented like a bird. Three months later they were married. Everybody said kind things; for you must know that Mrs Kilmarnock was not penniless herself. Oh, no! She lived in very good style in Torquay, and gave dinners that Torquay liked. And Torquay is a good judge of dinners. Her husband had been a Scottish Writer to the Signet, she said. So the marriage was celebrated amid universal plaudits, and there was quite three-quarters of a column about it in the *Western Morning News*."

At this juncture Carpentaria ventured to interrupt the speaker.

"You appear," he said, "to be remarkably well informed about matters which occurred long before you were of an age to take an intelligent interest in them. At the time of this marriage you surely were not in the habit of reading newspapers?"

"I was not," answered Jetsam drily. "I had attained the mature age of three years. If I am well informed it is because I have taken the trouble to inform myself. You see, I was interested, and I have spared no pains during this last year or two to acquire all the circumstantial details of the case."

"I perceive," said Carpentaria. "But how were you interested?"

"You will understand presently," said Jetsam. "To continue. This Mrs Kilmarnock, whom we must now call Mrs Ilam, used, both before and after her second marriage, to pay visits to the town of Teignmouth, and these visits were, not to put too fine a point on it, of an extremely discreet nature; they were, in fact, strictly secret. Mrs Ilam fell into the habit of telling her husband that she was going to Exeter to shop, but instead of going to Exeter she went only as far as Teignmouth. She was always dressed very simply indeed for these Teignmouth visits. She used to walk through the town from the station, and, having taken the ferry across the Teign, she walked up the right bank of the river till she came to a cottage that stood by itself in the marshy land thereabouts. At the cottage an old man and woman and a little boy would meet her. And the strange thing was that the old man spoke French; he could not speak English. You may possibly not be aware that onion-boats from the coast of Brittany are constantly arriving at the smaller Devonshire ports, such as Torquay and Teignmouth. The old man was a Breton peasant, with all the characteristics of a Breton peasant, who had arrived at Teignmouth once in an onion-boat, and forgotten to go back again because he fell in love with an Englishwoman – a Devonshire lass with a soft drawling accent. So Mrs Ilam used to talk to the Breton peasant in French, and to his wife in English, and to the boy in baby language. She would cover the boy with kisses; she would call him pet names, and she saw him at least once a week."

"He was her son?" Carpentaria put in interrogatively.

"You have naturally guessed it," Jetsam responded. "He was her son."

"But if she was really a widow, and this was really her son, why did she –"

"Oh," cried Jetsam, "I think she was really a widow, and there is not the slightest shadow of doubt that this was really her son. Perhaps she kept him a secret from Torquay because she felt that he might prove an obstacle to the achievement of her desires in Torquay. Anyhow, she loved him passionately. Her son was, beyond question, the greatest passion of her life." He turned abruptly again to the old woman, "Wasn't he?" he demanded.

And the aged creature's burning eyes were filled with tears.

"I think perhaps it might be as well to leave Mrs Ilam out of the conversation," suggested Carpentaria.

"Impossible to leave her out of the convocation," said Jetsam quickly, "because the conversation is almost exclusively about her. However, I will not trouble her any more for confirmation of what I say. Well, for nearly a year after her second marriage these clandestine visits of Mrs Ilam to the cottage on the banks, of the Teign continued with the most perfect regularity, and then something extremely remarkable happened."

"What was that?"

"First, I must tell you that soon after the marriage Mr Ilam's cataract got rapidly worse. In six months he could only distinguish objects vaguely. He could not read anything except shop signs. In Mrs Ilam he found an admirable nurse and companion. Except for her shopping excursions to Exeter she never left his side. She was a model wife, and all Torquay admitted the fact. Even when Mr Ilam's impaired vision rendered him captious, querulous, and indeed unbearable, she remained sweetness itself; and Mr Ilam would not admit any one but her to his presence. He even took a dislike to his child, his only son, and the infant was left in the charge of servants and governesses, except that Mrs Ilam saw him as frequently as she could."

"But this is not very remarkable," said Carpentaria, "such things are constantly happening."

"I am coming to the remarkable part," replied Jetsam, with a certain solemnity of manner. "One day the old Breton fisherman told Mrs Ilam that a relative had left him property in his native district, and that he had persuaded his wife to go with him to France so that they might end their days there. Mrs Ilam was extremely disturbed by this piece of news, because she did not know what to do with the boy. She asked the Frenchman how soon he proposed to leave, and the Frenchman said in about three weeks. She left and said she would come back again in a few days. It is at this point that the remarkable begins. Within a week all Torquay was made aware that Mr Ilam, at the solicitation of his wife, had decided to go to Paris to consult a great specialist there."

"I see," breathed Carpentaria, while Ilam's face wore at length a look of interest.

"I doubt if you do see," said Jetsam. "You think that Mrs Ilam was arranging to go to Paris in order to be nearer her son. Well, she was, but not at all in the way you imagine. They departed from Torquay almost at once, and in a somewhat remarkable manner, for Mrs Ilam dismissed every servant, even her own maid and Mr Ilam's man, and the child's nurse – all were dismissed in Torquay itself – and Mr Ilam and his wife and child left Torquay railway station entirely unaided, except by porters and the domestics of a hotel. Mrs Ilam would certainly have all her work cut out to conduct the expedition, for you must remember that at this period Mr Ilam was practically blind. Well, they had to change at Exeter and catch the Plymouth express, and at Exeter the old French peasant was waiting on the platform, evidently by arrangement, and he held Mrs Ilam's own little boy by the hand, and Mrs Ilam and the peasant had a long talk by themselves, and then the express came in, and the Ilams got into it, and the express started off again for London, and the French peasant was left standing on the platform holding the little boy by the hand. You see?"

"No," said Carpentaria bluntly.

"Well," proceeded Jetsam. "It was not the same little boy that the peasant held by the hand. Mrs Ilam had taken her own child with her, and left behind her step-child."

"Great heavens!" murmured Carpentaria.

"Exactly," said Jetsam. "Only the heavens didn't happen to interfere. This was no common case of substitution at birth, it was a monstrously ingenious change which Mrs Ilam, out of her passionate love for her own son, had planned and carried out in a manner suggested to her by the facts of the situation. Consider. The two boys were the same age – about three years – and they were dressed alike, Mrs Ilam had seen to that. Mr Ilam is nearly blind, certainly he could not distinguish one child of three from another child of three, even if they had been dressed differently. Moreover, Mr Ilam is not interested in the child. He is wrapped up in his own complaint, a ferocious egotist, like most sufferers. Probably the child sleeps during the journey to London – probably Mrs Ilam gives him something to make him sleep. The party arrive at Paddington, and are met by a new set of servants whom Mrs Ilam has engaged. She left Torquay with a child; she arrived at Padding-ton with a child. Who, except the old French peasant, is to know that there has been a change *en route*? The new child is kept entirely out of Mr Ilam's presence. He is taught his new name; he is taught to forget his past on the banks of the Teign; and he readily succeeds in doing so. His new nurse is suitably discreet. During their brief stay in London the Ilams stop at a hotel. They do not visit friends, on the plea of Mr Ilam's complaint. Then they leave London for Paris."

"The thing was perfect," observed Carpentaria, astounded.

"It was fatally perfect," Jetsam agreed. "Even had Mr Ilam been cured at once, the danger would have been but slight, because he had never seen his own child clearly. However, Mr Ilam was not cured at once, for it happened that the famous oculist whom they meant to consult died on the very day they entered Paris. It was seven years before Mr Ilam got himself cured; but in the end he was cured almost completely. The boy was then aged ten years. What possible chance was there of a discovery of the fraud? Even had Mr Ilam ever seen his child clearly, what resemblance is there between an infant of three and a boy of ten? None; none whatever. Mrs Ilam had triumphed: she had deposed the authentic heir of Mr Ilam and had put her own son on the throne in his stead."

"And the other boy?" Carpentaria queried.

Jetsam paused, his eyes bent downwards.

"Do you know the Breton peasantry?" he demanded suddenly, at length.

"Not in the least," said Carpentaria.

"Ah, well; that doesn't matter! When you hear the sequel of the story you will be able to imagine what a Breton peasant is capable of. He is the equal of the Norman peasant, and no French novelist has ever yet dared to write down the actual truth about the Norman peasant. I told you that Mrs Ilam and the old Frenchman had a chat on Exeter platform. She told him that she was giving him a new charge, preferring to take the other boy herself. It was arranged that the new charge should accompany the Breton to France, and live with him as his foster-child. Terms were fixed up, no doubt to the entire satisfaction of the peasant. Then Mrs Ilam ventured to play her great card. She informed the Frenchman that his new charge was a very delicate plant, frequently ill, and not apparently destined to long life. This, by the way, was grossly untrue. ' Of course, if he were to die,' she said in effect to the peasant, ' you would lose the income which I shall pay to you for looking after the child, and to compensate you for that loss I will promise to give you, if he dies, the sum of five hundred pounds.' I expect she managed to put a peculiar and sinister emphasis on these words. Anyhow, the Frenchman understood. That was just the kind of thing that you might rely on a Breton peasant to comprehend without too much explanation. Five hundred pounds is five hundred pounds; it is over twelve thousand francs, and twelve thousand francs to a Breton peasant is worth anything – it is worth eternal torture."

"And so, in due course, Mrs Ilam received news of her stepson's death?"

"In due course she received news of her stepson's death," said Jetsam. "It took a considerable time – six years, in fact – but it was accompanied by legal proof, and when she received it Mrs Ilam must have been as happy as the day is long, especially as her own boy was growing up strong and well, and Mr Ilam had taken quite a fancy to him. So all trace of the crime – would you call it a crime, or only a pleasing manifestation of a mother's love? – all trace of the crime was lost, for the French peasant died; the English wife of the French peasant had expired a long time before."

And Jetsam paused again.

"I am accepting all that you say as gospel," said Carpentaria. "Because somehow it impresses me vividly as being true." Here he looked at Josephus Ilam, who avoided his glance. "But how does the matter concern yourself, and in what way did you come upon the traces of the crime?"

"I'll tell you," Jetsam recommenced. "It was like this. The boy was not dead."

"Not dead? ""

"No. He had run away. He had had a pretty hard time before the death of the peasant's wife. Afterwards, his existence was a trifle more exciting than he could bear. He was starved and he was beaten. But that was not all. On board fishing-boats he was forced to accept dangers and risks of such a nature that the continuance of his life was nothing less than a daily miracle. So he ran away. He was aged nine, and he had a perfect knowledge of two languages as his stock-in-trade."

"But the legal proof of his death?"

"Nothing simpler. The foster-father was a great friend of the village schoolmaster, and the schoolmaster, as you may know, is always the secretary of the mayor in a French village. He it is who makes out all certificates, and transacts every bit of the routine business of population-recording. The foster-father suggested to the schoolmaster that in exchange for a certificate of the boy's death, the schoolmaster should receive a note of the Bank of France for a thousand francs. This was more than half a year's salary to the schoolmaster, and the result was that the foster-father got the certificate. No fear of discovery! None knew of the issue of the certificate except these two men. And the lady for whose benefit the certificate was issued would be extremely unlikely to visit a remote French fishing village."

"And what occurred to the boy?"

"The principal thing that occurred to the boy is that he is now sitting here and telling you his story," said Jetsam calmly.

"I guessed it," said Carpentaria, with equal calmness, "as soon as you mentioned that the boy was not dead."

Josephus Ilam maintained a stony silence.

"I knocked about for nine or ten years," continued Jetsam, "both in England and France, chiefly fishing. Then I suddenly became respectable. I got a place in a house-agency in Cannes, chiefly on the strength of my knowledge of French and English. Of course, that only lasted during the winter season. But my employer had a similar agency in Ostend during the summer. It was in Ostend that I became gay. I joined a theatrical troupe. I travelled a great deal. I did everything except make money. And after ten years of that I settled down again as a house-agency clerk. I really was rather good at that, much better than as a music-hall performer with revolvers, for instance. And in various ' pleasure cities' of Europe I acted as a clerk for over twenty years. Think of it – twenty years! And me growing older and narrower and more gloomy every year in the service of ' pleasure.' I never saved any money to speak of, even though I remained single, perhaps because I remained single. And then one day, finding myself at St. Malo, I thought I would go and have a look at that fishing village which I had fled from over thirty years before. My delightful foster-father was, of course, dead; so was the schoolmaster; but one or two people remembered me, and among them was an old woman who had been a charming young girl when I left. It appeared that my old foster-father had fallen deeply in love with her in a senile way, and at her parents' instigation she had married him for his money. He had confided to her, once when he thought he was dying, the secret of the substitution on Exeter platform. And now she told me. She had always liked me. You should have heard her pronounce ' Exeter.' It was the funniest thing."

Mr Jetsam laughed hardly.

"So that was how you got on the track?" said Carpentaria.

"Yes. I then pursued my inquiries in Torquay, and I found my old nurse. She told me that the real child of Mr Ilam had a large crimson birthmark on

the calf of his left leg. I had that mark. She also told me that there existed a photograph – one of the old daguerrotypes – of me as a child in the arms of my stepmother, my father standing close by, and that the mark on my leg was most clearly visible on this photograph. And that was the only real solid piece of information that I obtained, except that the photograph used to be kept in an old lacquered box. I had an instinct that the photograph had been preserved. And it was preserved – until to-night! I relied on the photograph. I could dimly recollect Torquay and Exeter platforms, but of what use would my assertions be without some proof, some tangible proof? When I thought of my wasted and spoiled and miserable life – and of what it might have been had I not been hated by a woman, I was filled with hatred and with – with such sorrow as you can't understand."

A sob escaped from Mr Jetsam, and Carpentaria got up and took his hand. "It is not too late for justice," said Carpentaria.

"That woman has always hated me," Jetsam murmured. "And even to-night her hatred still burned so fiercely that she tried to kill me. Even if she could speak, would she admit the truth? And she cannot speak."

"I think I can cause her to communicate with us," said Carpentaria. "You will see in a moment."

30

THE WORDS OF MRS ILAM

Carpentaria bent over the old woman, as if to search her eyes and find some kindness there.

And it seemed to him, indeed, that the character of her gaze had somewhat changed, though those brilliant orbs, famous in Torquay fifty years ago for their splendour, showed no trace of humidity.

Carpentaria himself was moved. It would have been impossible for any one, least of all an artist of romantic instincts such as he, to listen to Jetsam's recital without emotion. And now, when the narrative was finished, Jetsam sat silent and preoccupied, the figure of grief and of failure. One felt, in observing him, the immense tragedy of his life – a life which would not have been a tragedy, but merely a little slice of the commonplace, had he not by chance learned the sinister secret of his origin. One understood how the discovery of that secret had completely changed his view of existence, how it had filled him with ideas of frantic hope, frantic revenge, and frantic regret at the long drab irrecoverable years which the past had swallowed up. One penetrated, as it were, into his brain, and watched how he was continually contrasting what his career actually had been with what it might have been – with what it would have been but for the ruthless action of the woman on the bed.

And then there was the burly, smitten figure of Josephus Ilam, too, equally pathetic in its way. For love of this strong, heavy man, who once had been a little boy in a sailor suit standing on Exeter platform, the woman on the bed had committed a crime which was certainly worse than murder. She had made one life and she had marred another. And now she herself was stricken, withered, about to appear before the ultimate tribunal. It was incontrovertible that, if she had sinned, she had sinned magnificently, in the grand manner.

Carpentaria glanced at the two men, and then back again at the aged mother.

"I understand, Mrs Ilam," he began in a voice strangely soft and persuasive, "that you can indicate 'yes' or 'no' by a slight movement. Miss Dartmouth told me the other day. Is this so? I entreat you to answer me."

With a sudden jerk Josephus Ilam rose from his chair and rushed to the bedside.

"Answer him, mother."

Mother and son exchanged a long gaze, and then Mrs Ilam's eyelids blinked. It was the affirmative sign.

"Thank you," said Carpentaria simply. "Now it seems to me, if you are not too tired, that we can quite easily carry on a conversation upon this basis. It will be slow, but it will be none the less sure. By successively choosing letters out of the alphabet you can make up words, and so form sentences. You can choose the letters thus: I will run through the alphabet, and when I come to the letter you want, you will blink. Do you comprehend my scheme?"

The eyes blinked.

"And are you willing to try it?"

There was a considerable pause, but in the end the eyes blinked.

"Very good," said Carpentaria. "Now, quite probably you will want to begin with the letter ' I,' eh?"

The eyes blinked.

"Excellent! Your first word is ' I.' Let us go to the next word. A, B, C, D –"

At "D" the eyes blinked again.

With infinite patience, Carpentaria continued to help Mrs Ilam to express herself, and though that mouth was incapable of speech and those hands would never write again, the woman transmitted her first thought to the outer world, and it went thus:

"I do not regret."

There was something terrible, something majestic, in that unrepentant enunciation. It illustrated the remorseless character of the aged creature, whose spirit nothing apparently could conquer. Josephus Ilam moved away from the bed and hovered uncertainly between the dressing-table and the window. Jetsam got up from his chair and, taking Ilam's place, examined the features of the woman who had ruined his life and cheated him out of all that was his. And even Jetsam could not forbear an admiring exclamation.

"You are tremendous," he murmured. "I could almost like you."

Carpentaria waved him aside.

"Has Mr Jetsam told us the truth, dear madam?" he interrogated her.

And the eyes blinked. It was as though they blinked joyously, defiantly.

"Do you agree that restitution should be made, so far as restitution is possible?" Carpentaria asked.

There was no movement of the eyelids.

"You object to restitution, even now?"

Still there was no movement of the eyelids. But Josephus Ilam's legs could be heard shuffling on the floor.

"You wish to speak, then? A, B, C, D –"

Carpentaria went on to "W" before Mrs Ilam signified that the sentence was to commence. The words ran:

"Why named Jetsam?"

The woman's mind was evidently exploring, in a sort of indifferent curiosity, the side-issues, the minor scenes of the terrific drama which she had started and of which she now witnessed the climax. She appeared to have no sense at all of her own responsibility.

"It was a name I gave myself when I first found out who I was," said Jetsam bitterly. "Something chucked overboard and forgotten, you see."

A slight smile seemed to illuminate the woman's face.

"Do you agree that restitution should be made?" Carpentaria repeated patiently.

The eyes of the paralytic made no sign until Carpentaria began again to go through the alphabet. Then, letter by letter, the message came:

"If my son wishes."

"Mother," Ilam murmured, averting his face from the bed, "of course I wish. I nearly killed him myself the other day. You thought I had been dreaming – till you saw him yourself, and, and –"

He stopped; he broke down.

And then Mrs Ilam proceeded, with Carpentaria's help:

"My son must tell me about that."

"No," Jetsam put in authoritatively; "I will tell you about that. Ilam – or rather I should say Kilmarnock – is in no condition to make speeches.

When I first came to this place to begin my struggle for what was mine, I really had not got much of a plan in my head. It was so difficult to make a start.

It may seem to you quite a simple thing" – he turned away from Mrs Ilam and addressed Carpentaria –" to go up to a person and say to him, ' Look here, you are standing in my shoes, and your mother has committed an act foully criminal!' But in practice it isn't quite as easy as it seems. You want a gigantic nerve to make a statement like that as if you meant

it – although you do mean it. It sounds rather wild, you see.

And then I met my supplanter rather before I was ready for him. The truth is that he came into that little place where I was hiding in just the same way as you came in, Mr Carpentaria. He caught me like you did – a trespasser; and, of course, I was at a disadvantage. He spoke to me very roughly, and

then angered me –"

"How could I know who you were?" demanded Ilam.

"Exactly. You couldn't know. But the effect on me was the same. Put yourself in my place, Mr Kilmarnock. I had been cheated out of my whole career. You were in unlawful possession of it; and on the top of that you came along, and behaved to me as if I were a dog. Well" – here Jetsam addressed his stepmother again – "I told him who I was, and pretty quick too, and I could see from his manner that he knew the history of our origin, and the substitution on Exeter platform."

"I knew," Ilam admitted with a certain sadness." My mother had once told me – I came across traces of a mystery, and she told me."

"And you did nothing?" queried Jetsam. "It was not on your conscience?"

"You must recollect that we had the legal proof of your death. What was there to be done? I could not have made restitution to the dead, even had my mother permitted."

"But when I told you who I was," rejoined Mr Jetsam, "unless I am much mistaken, you believed what I said."

"I did," Ilam agreed. "Moreover, you bear a most distinct likeness to a portrait of my stepfather, painted when he was about your age."

"You believed me, and your answer was to try to kill me?" Jetsam sneered.

The two men, the son and the stepson, were now opposite to one another, on either side of the bed, while Carpentaria, intently listening, stood at the foot.

"I did not try to kill you," answered Ilam. "You pretty nearly succeeded," said Jetsam. "I thought I had killed you," Ilam said gravely. "But I had no intention of doing so. You said something very scathing about my mother –" "I said nothing that was not justified." "You insulted my mother. I lost my temper. I hated you. We always hate those whom we have wronged. I struck you. You fell, and you must have knocked your head against the pile of planks lying in the enclosure; you never moved. I examined you. I could have sworn you were dead – I was afraid – I thought of inquests. I knew the whole truth would come out. I had not meant to kill. So I took you and buried you temporarily, while I considered what I should do afterwards. I went back to the house and told my mother. She would not believe me. She thought I had been dreaming. I do frequently have bad nightmares. And certain things that occurred afterwards made even me suspect that after all I had been dreaming. It was not until you came again that I –"

"And even your mother believed then, eh?" said Jetsam. "Your mother believed too suddenly. She saw me and she believed! And the result was paralysis! I ought to have broken it to her more gently. That would have been perhaps better for all of us – perhaps better!"

There was a pause. And Jetsam added, as if communing with himself:

"How she hated me! How she hates me still! Even to-night, if some one had not interfered in time –"

He could not get away from the amazing tenacity of Mrs Ilam's purpose.

"You wish to speak?" said Carpentaria, who had been observing the woman's eyes; the eyes were blinking nervously.

He began the alphabet again, and her message ran thus:

"I do not hate him; but I love my son. To-night I thought Josephus was in danger. That was why – revolver. I always acted for my son. I love him!"

These sentiments, so unmistakably clear in their significance, took some time to transmit. Mrs Ilam appeared to be exhausted. But after a few moments she continued:

213

"Where is Rosie? She helped him. I want to know why."

The men exchanged glances.

"Why did she help you?" Carpentaria asked of Jetsam.

"Better ask her!" replied Jetsam curtly.

Carpentaria did not hesitate an instant. He went to the door, opened it, and called Rosie, and his voice resounded through the well of the staircase and the empty rooms. And then Rosie came from downstairs, like an apparition. She had been crying.

"Mrs Ilam wants you to explain why you have been helping Mr Jetsam," said Carpentaria, as she entered.

"Helping him in what?" Rosie parleyed timidly,

"In his plans –" "Against me," Ilam added.

"I only helped him in his plans for justice," said Rosie.

"But why?"

"Because I was sorry for him. Because there is something in his tone – because – oh! if he has told you all, are you not all sorry for him? When I think of what his life has been –" She stopped and burst into tears. "But my hair is grey," murmured Jetsam. "How can you possibly be interested in me? What does it matter what happens to me? My life is over."

"No it isn't!" Rosie protested. "It hasn't yet begun. It is just beginning. Mrs Ilam and Cousin Ilam will be just to you. You will not bear them ill-will. The wrong is too old for that. You will forget it. You will forget all the past. Your hair may be grey, but I'm sure your heart isn't. And your voice can influence even the Soudanese. The way that man obeyed you! The way he got the better of his brother just to please you! It seems strange, but I can understand it, because I have –" Again she stopped.

Jetsam went up to her and took her hand, which she seemed willingly to release to him. And he held it.

"How good you are!" he said steadily. "I am almost ashamed to have roused your sympathy so much."

The other two men watched.

"I don't know what Pauline will say," Rosie stammered.

Suddenly there was the sound of music. The band, which everybody in the room had forgotten, had begun to play, apparently of its own accord. And the melody it had chosen was, "See the Conquering Hero Comes."

Carpentaria rushed to the window. And then, as he drew the curtains, all noticed for the first time that the dawn had begun.

"What are you making that noise for?" he demanded angrily from the balcony. The music ceased abruptly.

"We're saluting the sun, sir," came the reply. "It's morning. We imagined that possibly you had lost sight of the fact of our existence."

"I had," said Carpentaria. "However, you can go!"

"Mr Carpentaria," cried another voice – a woman's, firm and imperious. "Open the front door immediately and let me in. I insist."

It was Pauline.

"Certainly, Miss Dartmouth," said Carpentaria obediently. "Kindly cut the rope which you will see tied to the handle. I will tell the Soudanese to admit you."

And he did so.

And presently footsteps were heard on the stairs, and both Pauline and Juliette came in.

"Rosie!" exclaimed Pauline. The sisters were clasped in each other's arms.

"Forgive me, dearest!" Rosie entreated; and they kissed.

"But what have you – ?" Pauline began, naturally mystified to the utmost.

"Ah, Miss Dartmouth," said Carpentaria, "I fear you must wait for enlightenment until you can hear the whole story."

"But the servants?" cried Pauline.

"I sent them to sleep in the staff-dormitories. I said you wished it," answered Rosie; smiling.

"But why should I wish it?"

"I don't know," said Rosie. "When they asked me that, I told

215

them I didn't know," she smiled again faintly. "But Mr Jetsam will explain it all to you. I – I tried to help him, and I have succeeded – I think."

During this conversation, Juliette, with that direct candour which frequently distinguishes women in a crisis, had gone straight to Josephus Ilam and seized his hand. She was assuring herself that he was not hurt, when Mrs Ilam once more gave a sign with her eyelids. Carpentaria resumed his position as helper.

"It was because I loved him," Carpentaria spelt out for her, "that I tried to kill you – twice."

Carpentaria fell back. Then he regained his self-command and, pushing his fingers through his red-gold hair, he asked monosyllabically, "Why?"

And then he interpreted for her the answer to his own question.

"You worried Josephus. He wanted to get rid of you."

Josephus disengaged his hands from those of Juliette.

"Mother!" he moaned sadly, and then added, "She is mad!"

But through Carpentaria Mrs Ilam said:

"I am not mad. But my love has always been too strong."

"Did you know of this, Ilam?" Carpentaria asked his partner solemnly.

"Of course I did not," was the answer – "not till it was too late."

"Then, why did you warn me up in the wheel?"

"Because I suspected. I suspected my poor mother was beginning to hate you, and I feared that – I can't say any more."

Carpentaria, powerfully moved, walked out of the room, and it was Pauline who followed him.

Mrs Ilam's eyes were now shut.

31

UNISON

That summer was astoundingly fine and warm, not to say tropical. But since it remains clearly in the memory of all, especially of the London water-companies, as a unique caprice on the part of the English climate, there is no need to go into details of its beauty. Towards the end of September the weather was exceedingly lovely. And of course the City prospered accordingly. It had been thought that the record "gates" during the great fetes of August would make the September returns look meagre and feeble. Such, however, was not the case. In the first week of September over a million people paid fifty thousand pounds at the turnstiles to enjoy the charms of the City. And a water-famine in most other parts of London did not impair their pleasure, for Ilam and Carpentaria had sunk their own artesian wells, and they had sunk them deep enough. Consequently, the glorious lawns of the Oriental Gardens and the turf of the cricket field kept a vivid green through that solitary summer.

The consumption of multi-coloured liquids in the cafes dotted about the gardens exceeded the most sanguine estimates. It was stated that during one of Carpentaria's concerts twelve thousand pints of Pilsen beer (the genuine article, imported daily in casks from the Erste Pilsen Actien-Brauerei, Pilsen) were consumed within sight of the bandstand.

"This," said Carpentaria emphatically, "is success. No composer-conductor," he added, "has ever before been able to say that he was listened to by an audience that put away Pilsen beer at the rate of a hundred pints a minute."

And he was right. Success was written large all over the place. Success shone on the faces of the entire staff, and it shone particularly on the face of Carpentaria, though he tried to pretend that it was nothing to him. It was, naturally, a great deal to him. He was the lion of London, and he knew it. All his previous triumphs were nothing in comparison with this triumph, which was the triumph of his ideas as well as a personal triumph.

Fifty amusement-mongers in London were asking themselves why they had not thought of building a City of Pleasure – and they were not getting satisfactory replies to the conundrum!

One evening, towards the middle of September, after a more than usually effective concert, Carpentaria laid down his baton on the plush cushion provided for its repose, and bowed and bowed and bowed again, in response to the enthusiastic plaudits, but with a somewhat preoccupied mien.

"What's up with the old man?" a French-horn player whispered to his mate.

"Dashed if I know!" replied the second French-horn player. "Unless he's in love."

"Well, he is," said the first. "Everybody knows that."

They called him the old man, no doubt, because his age was barely forty and because he looked younger than any of them.

Carpentaria descended from his throne, smiling absently at the applause of his band as he made his way through them to the steps leading down from the bandstand to the level of the gardens. He had only to move a few paces in order to be lost in the surging crowd. But before he could do this, he heard a voice:

"Mr Carpentaria."

He turned sharply. It was a woman's voice. It was more – it was Pauline's voice. Had she come to meet him? Impossible! That would have been too much happiness. However, he determined to ascertain, and he ascertained in his usual direct manner.

"Did you come especially to meet me?" he demanded.

And she replied, in a low voice:

"Yes."

"That was extremely kind of you," he said, trembling with joy.

"No," she protested. "I had something to tell you – and –" She hesitated, and then stopped.

"Suppose we take a little stroll," he suggested.

And she said, quite naturally:

"I should love to."

"This woman is simply the divinest creature," he told himself. "She is not like other women. She would like to go for a stroll with me, and she does not pretend the contrary. I am a great man, but I have done nothing, absolutely nothing, to deserve her goodness."

They crossed the gardens, with difficulty, in the direction of the terrace. And around were the light and laughter of the City – the brilliant illuminated cafes and the sombre trees for a background, and thousands of pretty toilettes and thousands of men gazing at the pretty toilettes, so attractive in the gloom under the starry sky. A burst of minor music would come now and then from some little cafe-orchestra, or the sound of the popping of guns from a distant shooting-gallery, or the roar of a lion, forced unwillingly to go through its performance in the menagerie. Then, every woman in the gardens gave a little start or a little shriek at the noise of the great cannon which signalled the commencement of the fireworks, and the rush to the terrace, where the best view was to be obtained, became a stampede.

"Do you mean to go on to the terrace?" asked Pauline.

219

"No, madam," said Carpentaria teasingly. "I mean to go on to the foreshore of the river. The tide is low – we shall be alone – we shall see both the crowd and the fireworks; and we shall be secure from interruption."

With one of his pass-keys, he unlocked a gate giving access to a tunnel leading down to the river. They passed through, and he locked the gate again. They arrived at the edge of the stream just as the first cluster of rockets was expanding itself in the firmament. The scene was impressive, and the roaring cheers of the serried crowd behind and above them did not detract from its impressiveness.?

"So you have something to tell me?" he remarked, tapping his foot idly against a stone. "I also have something to tell you."

"Really?" she answered.

He examined her face and figure. She was dressed in mourning, for Mrs Ilam had died within two days of the events set down in the previous chapter, and Carpentaria thought that black had never suited any woman so well as it suited Pauline… There was something about her face… In short… Well, those who have been through what Carpentaria was going through will readily understand.

"And what are you going to tell me?" he queried.

"It's a message from Cousin Ilam," said Pauline. "You haven't seen him to-day, have you?"

"No. I've been very much alone to-day. Juliette's been away all day – I suppose preparing for the wedding – there's only a few days left now."

"Well," said Pauline. "Cousin Ilam told me to tell you they aren't going to be married next week."

"What!" cried Carpentaria, "after all? Why not?"

"Because they were married this morning. They're already on their honeymoon."

"And Juliette has played this trick on me?" murmured Carpentaria.

"In any case, the marriage would have had to be very quiet," said Pauline. "I fancy Cousin Ilam didn't particularly care for your notion of having a section of your band to play at the church. Anyhow, he wanted the affair absolutely quiet. You know how nervous and self-conscious he is."

"Now I come to think of it," Carpentaria said, "Juliette did kiss me this morning rather fervently, and I wondered why."

"You wonder no longer," observed Pauline, smiling. "It was just a little plot."

"Extraordinary! Most extraordinary! "Carpentaria exclaimed.

"I don't think it's quite so extraordinary as all that!" said Pauline.

"You don't know what I mean," Carpentaria replied. "I also have a message – for you. It is from your friend Mr Jetsam Ilam and your sister. Have you seen Miss Rosie since this morning?"

"No," said Pauline; "she went with Juliette."

"Exactly. She went with Juliette. And she has done what Juliette has done. I was asked by Mr Jetsam Ilam to inform you that instead of marrying your sister next week he has married her this week. He is very sorry. He has a perfect horror of publicity. In fact they chose the registry office."

"What a shame!" cried Pauline. "What a shame!"

"Ah," said Carpentaria, "you didn't mind them deceiving me! But when it comes to deceiving you – ! It must have been a united plot on the part of those two pairs of people to deceive us two; and, I must say, they managed the thing pretty well. Don't you think so?"

"I think they've been horrid," said Pauline.

"And we two are quite alone, for one solid week – you in your house, and I in mine," said Carpentaria.

There was a pause, and then he heard a sob.

"You aren't really crying, are you?" he demanded.

Pauline made no answer.

221

In crying she had lost herself. She had given herself away –
she had precipitated a crisis which, in any event, could not have
been long postponed. In a word, he tried to comfort her. You
may guess how he did it. You may guess whether she objected.
You may guess if he succeeded. In a quarter of an hour she was
telling him that she had always liked him, that, formerly, she
and Rosie used to worship him – Rosie even more than she –
but that that sort of worship was nothing compared to the
feelings which she at present entertained – et seq.

And the fireworks and the applause of the vast crowd
provided the kind of setting that Carlos Carpentaria loved.

ARNOLD BENNETT

CLAYHANGER

In this, the first volume of an ambitious series intending to trace the parallel lives of a man and woman from youth to marriage and from marriage to old age, Bennett introduces the character of Edwin Clayhanger. A sober portrait of a boy growing up under a tyrannical father contrasts with young Edwin's glimpses of the mysterious and tantalizing Hilda Lessways. As the lives of these two characters unfold before us, Bennett uses autobiographical detail to beautifully depict the constraints and spiritual adventures of young life in the Potteries.

HILDA LESSWAYS

In the second volume of the Clayhanger series, events in *Clayhanger* are retold from the perspective of Hilda Lessways, who is embarking on a relationship with Cannon, a charismatic entrepreneur, whose success has taken him from the Five Towns to Brighton. As Hilda's fascination with the young Clayhanger grows, one of Bennett's most living heroines must face up to her conflicting emotions, and the reality of her hopes and tragedies.

Arnold Bennett

These Twain

In *Clayhanger* and *Hilda Lessways*, Bennett followed the development of a relationship from two very different perspectives. He now draws these perspectives together in a gripping novel which sees the two young protagonists embarking upon married life. One might expect a fairy tale romance, but both Edwin and Hilda are extremely strong-willed, and this clash of personalities makes for a marriage that often hovers on the brink of failure.

This volume of the Clayhanger series contains some of Bennett's very finest work, depicting superb scenes from provincial life and painting a powerful picture of the conflict of wills in an inharmonious marriage.

The Roll Call

The final volume of the Clayhanger series sees Hilda's son, George Cannon (who quickly changes his name from Clayhanger), as an architect, in many ways representing the ambitions held by his stepfather Edwin Clayhanger. However, he possesses an arrogance endowed by family wealth and Bennett examines the difficulty of bringing up children without spoiling them with some aplomb. It is a riveting tale which sees George eventually in the army and a fitting finale to one of the finest series in English literature.

A Man from the North

Fleeing a drab and dead ' existence, Richard Larch moves south from Bursley t.   ...on, intent on pursuing a career as a writer. He is also looking for companionship and love, but finds his high hopes dashed when life in the capital is fraught with difficulties, and the glittering career proves to be more elusive than anticipated.

Melancholic and starkly realistic, *A Man from the North* is Arnold Bennett's first novel.

The Old Wives' Tale

Arnold Bennett's masterpiece, *The Old Wives' Tale*, chronicles the lives of sisters Constance and Sophia Baines, daughters of a Bursley draper. Constance, a conventional and sombre young woman, marries the shop's chief assistant, while the spirited and adventurous Sophia elopes to Paris with Gerald Scales, an irresistible but unprincipled cad. This is the utterly compelling story of their lives and loves, their triumphs and despair from early teens to old age, told with Arnold Bennett's characteristic insight and truthfulness.

How to Live on 24 Hours a Day

'You have to live on...twenty-four hours of daily time. Out of it you have to spin health, pleasure, money, content, respect, and the evolution of your immortal soul'.

This timeless classic is one of the first 'self-help' books ever written and was a best-seller in both England and America. It remains as useful today as when it was written, and offers fresh and practical advice on how to make the most of 'the daily miracle' of life.